The Woman

Who Cut

Off Her

Leg *at the*

Maidstone

Club *and*

Other Stories

Praise for Julia Slavin's
The Woman Who Cut Off Her Leg at the Maidstone Club
and Other Stories

"This is the most singular and arresting collection of short fiction I've read in years. Based on the reading experience, which is two-thirds delight and one-third windowpane LSD, you'd think Slavin injected DNA from Bruno Schulz's moldering skeleton, but I think the even more amazing and inspiring truth is that she came up with these stunning pages on her own. Who knows how these things happen? Just read it."
—Rick Moody, author of *The Ice Storm*

"It is a collection of short stories that are, individually and together, improbable, outrageous, fanciful, captivating, and somehow for all their horrific touches of surrealism very, very cheerful.... The success of Slavin's prose seems to me to ride on its unrelenting naturalness. She is an extraordinarily attentive and selective—and subtle reporter. Details are lean, precise, uncluttered, fine-edged tapestry weaving."
—*The Baltimore Sun*

"I'd have sworn I could hear John Cheever laughing. Julia Slavin is astonishing."
—Susan Dodd, author of *The Mourner's Bench*

"The writing in this collection of twelve stories sparkles.... Slavin is a truly gifted writer. She's funny and precise and has a very dry wit. This book had me enraptured all the way through and dreading its final page: a rare response to a collection of American short fiction these days."
—*The Cleveland Plain Dealer*

"[These stories] bubble up out of a quietly desperate, normalized insanity that has a brave tradition in literature and that I believe will be good fuel for the rocket ship that will take us to the new planet."
—Susan Salter Reynolds, *Newsday*

"These stories move from the mundane to the surreal, sometimes abruptly, sometimes gradually, but always with intelligence, wiliness, and wit."
—*The Boston Globe*

"Slavin takes her perceptions beyond the natural world's limits; she's wildly inventive and drolly post-ironic."
—*Seattle Times/Post Intelligencer*

"Punky, hilarious, [and] provocative." —*New York Observer*

"Sparkling...surreal...The bittersweet irony of these stories lies in the revelation that love, reduced to a simple physical state, is just as complicated, painful, and difficult as love in its evanescent form."
—Judy Budnitz, *The Village Voice*

"Slavin is a gutsy writer, unafraid to make dreamlike leaps of logic or to exploit potent psychosexual imagery."
—*Time Out New York*

"Slavin's talent is close to perfection."—*Arizona Daily Star*

"Slavin's style is simple, clean, reminiscent in tone of fairy tales, yet her characters are quite well developed, and her insights into the complexities of the human heart are thought provoking. True love, adultery, incest, marriage, jealousy, the joys of parenthood—all figure here, larger than life and skillfully portrayed. This is one must-read collection of short stories."
—*Booklist* (starred review)

"There is nothing predictable about Slavin's work; by turns charming and eerie, her stories are sure to engage and stimulate. Highly recommended."
—*Library Journal* (starred review)

The Woman Who Cut Off Her Leg *at the* Maidstone Club *and* Other Stories

Julia Slavin

PICADOR USA
A John Macrae Book
Henry Holt and Company
New York

THE WOMAN WHO CUT OFF HER LEG AT THE MAIDSTONE CLUB AND OTHER STORIES. Copyright © 1999 by Julia Slavin. All rights reserved. Printed in the United States of America. No part of this book may be used or reproduced in any manner whatsoever without written permission except in the case of brief quotations embodied in critical articles or reviews. For information, address Picador USA, 175 Fifth Avenue, New York, N.Y. 10010.

Picador® is a U.S. registered trademark and is used by Henry Holt and Company under license from Pan Books Limited.

For information on Picador USA Reading Group Guides, as well as ordering, please contact the Trade Marketing department at St. Martin's Press.
Phone: 1-800-221-7945 extension 763
Fax: 212-677-7456
E-mail: trademarketing@stmartins.com

Some of these stories were published in slightly different form in the following: *Arkansas Review:* "Painting House." *Crescent Review:* "Swallowed Whole" and "Dentaphilia." *Fence:* "The Woman Who Cut Off Her Leg at the Maidstone Club" (originally titled "Maisie's Foot"). *Gargoyle:* "Beauty and Rudy." *Pushcart XXII:* "Dentaphilia." *Story:* "Pudding."

Designed by Michelle McMillian

Library of Congress Cataloging-in-Publication Data

Slavin, Julia.
   The woman who cut off her leg at the Maidstone Club and other stories / Julia Slavin.
     p.   cm.
   Contents: Swallowed whole—Babyproofing—Dentaphilia—The woman who cut off her leg at the Maidstone Club—Covered—Beauty and Rudy—Rare is a cold red center—Pudding—Lives of the invertebrates—Blighted—Painting house—He came apart.
   ISBN 0-312-26413-5
   1. United States—Social life and customs—20th century—Fiction.
   I. Title.
PS3569.L296W66 1999   98-50765
813'.54—dc21   CIP

First published in the United States by Henry Holt and Company

First Picador USA Edition: July 2000

10 9 8 7 6 5 4 3 2 1

For Jack More, Jesse Thomas,
and John Christopher Arnholz

Acknowledgments

For their astounding support I am grateful to the Tabard Group: Jan Linley, Fiona J. Mackintosh, and Beth Millemann. I also wish to thank Esther Newberg, Jeff Jackson, Denise Shannon, Rachel Klauber-Speiden, and my editor, Jack Macrae. Thanks to my parents. Thanks to Dan Slavin and Paul Slavin. And for guidance and honesty, Claudia Rosenthal Plepler.

Contents

The Woman

Who Cut

Off Her

Leg *at the*

Maidstone

Club *and*

Other Stories

Swallowed Whole

There's a way young skin looks that no amount of plastic surgery can recapture. It has an unmarred translucence, as though the flesh were stretched under a fluorescent street-lamp. But I think it was the little red baseball cap he wore backward, like a catcher, that sent me off my feet.

His name was Chris. He mowed our lawn.

As he worked, I moved window to window watching him cut our grass in horizontal rows. His edges were uneven, but I didn't give a damn, they were his, and after he was gone I lay outside, patted the bristly blades like a new haircut, and said, You are my lawn. Today a beautiful boy cut you and edged you.

It was a late July afternoon. The sky was blue and cloudless. The sun was just dipping behind the maple in the McNaultys' yard. He leaned against the back doorframe with his thumbs in the pockets of his long shorts, his shirt tied through a belt loop, MONTANA written across his belt in blue and white beads.

"Would you like to come out and see?"

"No, I trust you." I was relieved I could still talk.

"Are you sure?" He leaned into the kitchen. "Customer satisfaction is our number-one concern."

Everything I was thinking was wrong and dangerous. I paid him for the lawn and scooted him out the back. This is like being sick, I thought, holding a bottle of San Pellegrino to my forehead. I've contracted a lawn virus named Chris. I didn't know how I was going to wait ten days for our lawn to grow.

I put up a pot of decaf and called the drugstore for another prescription of Clomid, the fertility drug I was taking. Then I put on Sibelius and sat down to dress my loom. I threw the heddle under the weft and was gliding along smoothly when the smell of dirt and grass came over me like a soft blanket. I raced out of the house. Maybe I could sweat him out of me. I heard the sound of mowers everywhere and ran to them, praying one would be Chris's. I was the mercury from a broken thermometer, bouncing off the sidewalks, zigzagging the neighborhood, mower to mower.

Chris looked up from the Leonards' lawn where he was crouching, pulling the mower cord to get the engine started. "Hello, Mrs. Carter," he said.

"Chris," I said. "I was wondering . . ."

He stood up, took a pack of Camels out of his pocket, and

shook one out. He offered me a cigarette and I took one. He struck a match, cupped grass-stained hands around it, and held it for me. I hadn't smoked in eight years.

"Yes?" he said. "You were wondering?"

"I was wondering if you did other things—you know, besides mowing, like weeding and clipping."

"I have," he said. "Done those things. In the past."

"Would you then?" I said. "For me?"

"I could give you an estimate." He put his hands on my ass.

"Not here."

"Why not?"

He stuck his tongue in my mouth. I sucked on it. I didn't care who saw. I sucked his tongue and he started to moan because I was hurting him, but that just made me suck harder. He tried to push me away. I sucked harder. He started to scream. His mouth was wide open, his eyes looked like they were going to bug out of his head, his tongue hit my uvula, and I sucked him down my throat. All of him. As I watched his feet lift off the ground and follow the rest of him down my gullet I thought it was kind of funny, but once he was in, I felt my rib cage expand and numbing pain all over my body. I was certain my chest was going to explode and I couldn't breathe. I collapsed on the grass and lay on my back waiting to die. "Help, help," I could only whisper.

"Look what you've done," Chris screamed inside me.

"Help, help," I whispered.

"Help, help," Chris mimicked. He rearranged himself to take the pressure out of my chest, but when he moved, his elbow jabbed into my pancreas and I screamed. Then he settled farther down in me, and though I still couldn't move, it wasn't quite as painful anymore. I managed to roll onto my knees and pull myself up with the handle of the mower. Once I was standing I thought I was going to sink into the ground. I couldn't remember how to walk.

"Left foot, right foot," Chris said. I put my left foot out and dragged my right foot to meet my left. Every step I took felt like I had to climb over a hurdle sideways. I used the mower as a walker and waddled home with my legs apart as if I'd just gotten off a horse.

"We're going to go call my husband and figure this out," I said. Chris didn't answer. He'd gone to sleep.

"Ready?" I said, kneeling in front of the toilet.

"Hang on," Chris said, and I felt my sides cinch together.

"Chris, honey. Every time you move it feels like being run over by a truck."

"I'm trying to get my arms in."

"You're hurting me."

"You did this!"

"You just prepare yourself to get out." I stuck my finger in my throat. I was good at purging. I had a bulimarexia period in college and still resorted to the old heave-ho after a big meal from time to time. The gag reflex set in right away. I felt my saliva thin and that familiar contraction in my stomach right before I'm about to spill. But instead of blowing, I felt a guttural moan coming from deep within me.

"Stop," Chris said. "You're killing me."

"What happened?"

"My neck. I think it's broken. You pulled it."

"Stay calm. Try to move your head."

"I thought you weren't supposed to move a broken neck," he said. "You know, until the emergency rescue workers get here."

"Move it," I said. At first I felt nothing and I thought that maybe I *had* broken his neck, but then he banged his head up against my solar plexus. It felt like I'd been punched by a heavyweight champ.

"Not broken," Chris said.

I wanted him out of me. I didn't care if he came out in pieces, I wanted him out. I stuck my hand in my mouth and down into my throat. With Chris screaming in my stomach, I puked up undigested hummus and cucumber on pita, some of the morning's Special K, and a little spaghetti carbonara from the night before. But then something came out of my throat that I didn't quite recognize, a taste from long ago: charcoaled, greasy, and rich. I looked in the toilet at brown vomit, veined with little red and yellow capillaries of ketchup and mustard. There was even a small green circle of pickle. I'd thrown up Chris's lunch.

"Where the hell are you?" It was my husband, Bruce, on the phone. I'd forgotten this was the night of the firm dinner.

"I'm so sorry," I said. "I got carried away on the loom and forgot to watch the clock."

"Just get here," Bruce said. "Speed if you have to. The firm'll pay for the ticket."

I rifled through the closet looking for something that wasn't too sexy or too dowdy that the other spouses and partners hadn't seen before, and came up with a navy blue silk shift and a pair of tan mules. I packed a tube of lipstick and a perfume atomizer in a small Chanel bag, threw it in the back of the Saab, peeled out of the driveway, and floored it around the curvy roads of the parkway. At the zoo exit I tasted hamburger again.

Bruce met me at the door. "I'm really sorry," I said.

"It's all right. I'm just glad you're here. Everyone's excited to see you."

I looked at the long table of partners and spouses and quickly tried to remember everyone's name. "Randi, Dan, nice to see you. Carol, Trey; Mr. Westin"—the senior partner—"so sorry to be late. I'm going to *sue* our mechanic." Everyone laughed. "Mrs. Westin, so nice to see you. Bill, Sheryl. I love that scarf; is it Hermès?"

"Blah, blah, blah," Chris said, nearly scaring me out of my mules. "When do we eat?"

A place card with my name on it was directly across from the senior partner's wife. "Getting acclimated to being in the suburbs, Sally?" Mrs. Westin asked.

"Nice of you to remember," I said. "I'd love for you and Mr. Westin to come over. We bought one of the old Sears kit homes in Section Five . . . *ah!*" I felt a sharp pain.

"Feel my boner?" Chris said.

I looked down and saw the little tent effect of my dress from Chris's erection sticking out above my belly button. He began moving it up and down my abdominal viscera.

"Talked to the Texas Group again," Dan Weiser said. "Those cowboys made a fortune. All their assets were underwater, but the New York group got them incredible execution."

Bruce held up his hands. "Well, Dan, that's the magic of structured finance."

"And here's where it really gets sexy. . . ." Dan continued.

"This feels great," Chris said. "Tighten your abs."

"Shhh."

"So, Sally," Sheryl Arlen said. "Still no kiddies?" She reached across Dan Weiser and patted my belly.

"Oh," I said, sadly. "We're still working on it."

"Working *hard?*" Sheryl winked.

"Contract your abs," Chris said, jamming into my stomach muscles. "Contract, contract." Chris was bucking so hard I bounced up and down in my chair. I grabbed my seat to steady myself.

"Stop it."

"It's too good. Your vena cava's so tight."

"Are you working outside the home, Sally?" Mrs. Westin asked, cutting into roast garlic duck.

"I'm working," I said, hanging on for dear life to my chair. "I'm not getting paid, but I'm working." My voice was quivering uncontrollably, like sitting on a vibrating platform. "You know, working on the house, working at the loom."

"Contract, contract, tighter, tighter." Chris made one final thrust that forced me up out of my chair. I put my hands out to stop myself. I hit the table with a smack and spilled all the water glasses. Then a projectile of semen shot out of my mouth, flew across the table, and covered Mrs. Westin's duck like a fruit glaze.

`   `   `

Chris always slept until noon, so I had some time to myself to read the paper and work at my loom. But then he'd wake up with a huge morning erection. "Not the liver," I'd say, and Chris would find some cavity to enter or another organ or muscle to hump. He'd been in me for two weeks, and I must say I was getting used to having him. I loved my husband, I really did, but now that Bruce and I were having sex procreatively, it seemed like such a chore. Besides, Chris seemed to enjoy our sex so much. He was so complimentary and appreciative when I tightened my abs or twisted back and forth at the waist that I couldn't resist.

One night Bruce was working late so we went to a little French place downtown. "I'll have the grilled vegetable plate," I told the waitress.

"And a cheeseburger," Chris said.

"And a cheeseburger."

"And an omelet. And get some of those skinny fries French people make. And a milkshake. And some of those pastries on the cart."

"I can't eat all that," I whispered.

"You're too bony," he said. "I want you plumper."

"And some of those lovely fries," I told the waitress.

"Let's get wine," Chris said.

"And a carafe of your house red."

"I was thinking about the first time I saw you," Chris said, over an after-dinner cigarette I smoked for us.

"What did you think?"

"I wished I were older," he said. "I wished you weren't married. I thought you were beautiful."

"You're drunk."

"Yes." He put his hands behind my breasts.

"Not here."

"I just want to have my hands here. I'm not going to do anything." I felt his hands slide down the back of my ribs as he fell asleep. I ordered a plum tart so he would have a treat waiting for him when he woke up. I'd forgotten how much teenagers need to sleep.

I was dreaming that Chris was outside me kissing my neck and opened my eyes to Bruce. He dragged his tongue from my neck down my body. When he got to my hips he moved my legs apart and put his head between them.

"Oh, Bruce," I moaned.

Bruce shot up in bed and screamed.

"What?" I said. "What is it?"

He backed away from the bed. "There's a . . . there's an eye!"

I rushed to Bruce, who was slumped down in the corner.

"Sally, I'm sorry," he whimpered. "I'm really under the gun at work. I'm trying to get some time off so we can go away together. I've been a bad husband lately."

"No, no, no." I took my husband in my arms and rocked him. "It's me who's been bad." Bruce put his arms around me. I knew what I had to do.

"I'm not going," Chris said.

"We need our life together back," I said. "This arrangement is eating away at everything."

"I won't go," he said.

"You're a nice kid. You should be going on dates with girls and playing baseball."

"No. I want to be with you. I won't go." He wrapped his arms around my large intestine.

"Chris, if you won't go yourself, I'm going to have to make you go."

"No, you won't. I know something you don't know: You're pregnant."

I put my hand over my mouth. Of course. I'd been so distracted by Chris I hadn't noticed my period was late. I ran to the phone to call Bruce with the news.

"Put down the phone," Chris said. "The child is mine."

"You're wrong," I said. "I've been taking my temperature. Bruce and I have kept to the schedule."

"His sperm never got past me," Chris said. "I swallowed it."

"You . . . you little prick." I belted myself in the gut. "You're lying."

"You've got enough of my sperm in you to create a battalion. What do you think I do in here all day? The child is mine." He cupped my uterus in his hands and chanted, "I am the father. I am the father."

"Bruce, the most wonderful news," I said on the phone.

"I am the father."

"Really?" Bruce cried. "I'll be right home."

"What are you going to tell Bruce when the kid only grows to be five-two with a big head?" Chris said, as I stacked fresh towels in the linen closet.

"You'll grow into your head."

"I'm full grown," Chris said. "My dad has a big head and his dad had a big head and my mom has a big head too."

Bruce and I had a beautiful evening, which we hadn't had in a long time. We went for a walk in the park and sat out back on the deck and ate cherries. I begged Chris to go to sleep so we could be alone, and he did.

"You're going to have to stop singing that song," I told Chris one morning at my loom. Chris only slept when I slept now so I never had any time alone anymore. He was always singing bad music and moving around and he had to eat all the time. I felt fat and exhausted.

"It's Lizard Savior. It's great music."

I threw the shuttle back and forth through the shed.

"That's not music," I said. "Beethoven is music. Mozart is music."

"That's boring music. And you think it's boring too, if only you'd admit it."

"Your Lizard Saviors are insipid."

"What's insipid mean?"

The shuttle got tangled in the weft and I got a yarn burn on my thumb. *"Ouch,* dammit. I need some time alone. Go to sleep."

"I'm not tired." He tickled an ovary with his boner.

"I'm not in the mood."

"You never are these days." He entered my ileum.

I tried drinking a pitcher of ice water, but by the time it made its way through my pharynx and esophagus, it sprinkled on Chris's head like a warm shower. I thought of downing a pint of Wild Turkey to put him out but I was worried about harming the fetus. My hands were tied. He could do whatever he wanted.

"I want him to play football," Chris said, pulling out of my appendix.

"No child of mine is playing football. Too dangerous. He can play baseball. Anyway, what if it's a girl?"

"It's a boy." I put my hand on my middle and started to cry. I was carrying a boy, a son.

Early the next morning a soft trembling in my belly woke me. Chris was crying.

"Chris?" I felt around for his head, found it resting on top of my uterus, and patted it through my skin. "What's the matter?"

"You're having a miscarriage," he said, and wept. I wrapped my arms around myself. "Five o'clock today. The baby's dead."

"What happened?"

"Defective implantation," he said.

"All your moving around. You did this."

"No!" he cried.

"You've been fucking me all over the place. I knew it was dangerous."

"It was my child too. I know you feel bad, but I feel just as bad."

"You don't have any idea how I feel." I ran down to the kitchen.

"Yes, I do. I feel everything you feel."

"I want you out. Get out now."

"Never."

I tore open the cabinet under the sink, yanked out a bottle of Formula 409, unscrewed the cap, and tilted my head back. I didn't care if it killed us both.

Around two in the afternoon I woke up on the couch. I'd spent the morning puking 409.

"Aw, morning sickness," Bruce had said, as he headed out the door. "Don't worry about me, I'll get the bus."

I tried to sit up. The room was still spinning from the household cleaner, but I was alive. I felt myself for Chris but there was nothing. Nothing. I put my face in the couch and cried. "Chris, Chris, come back. Please. I'm sorry. Give me another chance." Then I felt the stirring in my pelvis that had become so familiar and comfortable these past few months. I wrapped my arms around my waist. "Chris? Chris, are you all right?"

"Huh?" He was groggy but alive. "Yeah, the cleaner mixed with your stomach acid worked as a pretty strong hallucinogenic. I saw a jade Buddha sitting on your colon. I guess you're pretty disgusted with me at this point."

"No. I'm happy to feel you. I'm sorry if I hurt you."

"Let's go to sleep." He rubbed the back of my belly, which made me drop off quickly.

I woke up again at six and knew by the lightness I felt that Chris was out of me. I stood up and felt like I could float. I unzipped the bloody slipcovers off the couch and went upstairs to wash up and change. Everything was quiet and peaceful, and I walked through my house alone. Outside,

Chris emptied the grass cage of his mower into a lawn and leaf bag. Later, I heard his mower over at the Leonards' house join the chorus of other mowers in the neighborhood, but I can always pick out Chris's. It's the one that's low, sweet, and unwavering, like a lover's voice.

Babyproofing

My wife dreams the pantry shelves buckle and the baby is buried under a thousand cans of beans. She dreams Caroline gets sucked into the chimney; we can hear her gurgle and sing softly to herself—"Rock of Ages," to be exact—but we can't get to her. We don't even know what chimney to look up because, in the dream, the house has twenty, thirty chimneys and more keep popping up—*bing! bing! bing!*—through the roof. She dreams the baby falls out the second-floor window. She could catch her if she could get outside in time, but something grabs at her ankles. An enormous lobster claw pulls her down into the floor, below the foundation, and by now she's jerked herself awake. It's me that's holding her ankles, holding her down. I'm the claw, right?

"No, Walter, not every bad dream is about you." She moves away from me, swinging her legs over the side of the bed and stepping around the porta crib, where the baby still sleeps after all these months despite my insistence she sleep in her own room. "Look deeper," she calls in a whisper, over the tinny alto of her urine hitting water.

I don't think about dreams. Once a year, when the annual report is due, I dream that my father is a Greek shipping magnate, sailing on the open sea in his magnificent vessel, and I'm bobbing around in a dinghy tied to the back.

Sarah returns to bed but can't get back to sleep; she's worrying about the Casablanca fans coming loose from the ceiling. I've checked them, I tell her. I've hung from the poles. I've done chin-ups on those fans. She tries warm milk. She pees again. We lie awake thinking about ceiling fans falling down and what they could do to a nine-month-old.

Mitzy Baker, president and CEO of Baby Safe, Inc., stands in the center of our living room, taking everything in like an admiral on the deck of his flagship. Right away I remember the fireplace equipment that hangs over the marble like huge dental tools, the drop-leaf maple table my great-grandfather smuggled out of Russia, the Sunufu fertility statue teetering on the low oak stand.

"I know about the fireplace equipment and the table," I blurt out.

Mitzy Baker manages a phony grin that mirrors the smiling kittens embroidered on her cashmere sweater set. Her starched hair is pulled into a matching kitten band that seems to be pulling everything up; her face, her mouth, her neck, even her shoulders are too close to her ears.

Now and then she gives an obligatory smile to the baby. But Caroline's not falling for it. She wrinkles her eyebrows and drools. That's my girl.

"Incidentals," Mitzy Baker says. "Those are the easy things. The table, the fireplace equipment, the art, these sharp edges." She points to our glass coffee table with the point of a navy patent-leather pump and writes something down on a clipboard. Any minute the Gestapo will bust through the door and whisk Sarah and me off to the basement of a building where we'll be judged by a panel of babies in fiberglass bike helmets. What do I feel so guilty about? I called *them,* didn't I?

We go into the library. I know the bookshelves are wrong. I don't need Mitzy Baker to tell me the baby could pull them down on top of herself. Yes, I could have spent twenty-five cents on an elbow joint and attached the shelves to the wall before this chilly, judgmental woman came into our home. But I've been busy with work and Sarah with the baby and that's what I'm considering hiring Baby Safe to do, right? She shakes the shelves to see just how unsteady they are, how reckless we are, how we care more about the beauty of our house than the safety of our child, and writes something else down on that blasted clipboard.

"Incidentally," Mitzy Baker says, "a head could get stuck in here." With her blue pump, she points to a space in the wrought-iron banister we had made in Virginia.

"I'm not pulling out the banister," I whisper to Sarah. "We spent two thousand dollars on that banister."

"What do you suggest?" Sarah asks. "Should we replace it?"

"No," I say. "The baby's just going to have to learn not to stick her head in there."

Mitzy Baker stares at me for a moment. Something's clipped the wire that keeps my posture straight. I feel myself slouch two inches. "Again," she says. "The banister is an incidental. We fix it."

She manages a nice subservient smile. I rise back up to my full six feet two.

"Have you thought of covering the floors?" Mitzy Baker asks, tapping her shoe on the hardwood in the living room. "My pediatric neurologist friend says head injuries are what put his kids through college."

Sarah squirms. The thought of head injuries, along with faceless baby snatchers in black vans with no license plates, keeps her up at night.

"Covering the floors with what?" I ask.

"We have a three-inch rubber padding. It's firm but has give. It comes in taupe, wheat, cobalt, and toffee. It's a wonderful product and not unattractive."

Sounds beautiful.

"May I?" she asks, gesturing toward one of our Moser dining chairs.

"Please," Sarah says.

Mitzy Baker sits at our Moser table, takes a calculator from an accordion envelope, and gets to work on the clipboard. She pivots her sharp heel back and forth on our newly refinished wood floor while she pecks out numbers. The calculator adds and advances, making sounds like a sick man clearing his throat. I wait for her to move her foot aside to see if she's left a mark. She pauses for a moment to look around the dining room.

"Lovely table." She taps on the cherry wood with a white frosted fingernail. "Is it Swedish?"

"It's from Maine," I say. It's a *Moser,* for Chrissake.

Ten minutes later, after Sarah and I have been throwing glances at each other, arguing with our eyebrows, shrugging and clasping our hands and offering coffee that keeps getting refused, Mitzy Baker puts her pen down, laces her fingers together to make a shelf for her starched head, and rests her chin on her hands.

"What do you worry about, Mrs. Peel, at night, lying in bed?" Her voice is gentle. "What's your fantasy? What's the worst thing that can happen?"

A tear splashes on the Moser table. I move over to my wife, but it's Mitzy Baker's hand that Sarah takes.

"Shhhh. Putting words to the feeling will make it better."

"I can't stop thinking about—"

"Let's stop this," I say.

"No." Sarah slides my hand off her shoulder. She straightens in her chair. "There were those girls who disappeared. Their mother went inside to get sweaters—" Sarah breaks down.

"The Whiley sisters," I say. "That was twenty years ago."

"Those things happen, yes." Mitzy Baker's hand smooths my wife's hair. "But rarely, so rarely. Your house, Mrs. Peel, is your daughter's worst enemy." Sarah picks up her head. "We are dealing with a weapon here, Mrs. Peel. A dangerous weapon."

I look over at Caroline, sitting on the entrance hall floor, gumming the blue rings of her Wiggle Worm. "What's the bottom line?" I ask, rubbing my thumb and index finger together.

The women look at me like I'm Goebbels. Then Mitzy Baker looks down at the clipboard, as if she doesn't have the price tag recorded on her synapses.

"Give us complete access and control of your house, Mr. and Mrs. Peel. For three days your house is my house. We'll create a safe haven for your little one."

I look over her shoulder at the grand total. "Four thousand dollars?"

"It's a very good deal if you break it down into hours and manpower. We leave no stone unturned—and believe me, neither will your daughter if you don't do some serious babyproofing." She looks up toward the attic as though the place has a terrible secret. Then she looks sadly over at Caroline, who's pulled herself up on the glass coffee table. We've been so busy thinking about how to keep her alive, we missed the first time she ever stood up by herself.

"All I wanted was a couple of cabinets locked and some gates on the stairs," I say to Sarah, as we watch Mitzy Baker stroll down the front walk of the house.

"These are lovely trees," Mitzy Baker calls back to us, looking up at the beeches. "They must be ancient."

"We like them too," I call back. Two squirrels spiral their way up a trunk and disappear into the deep foliage. A cardinal mom comes in for a landing with dinner. "Preposterous," I say to Sarah. "Sheer and utter crap."

"*Someone* must be buying into this crap," Sarah says, as we watch Mitzy Baker slide into her leather-smothered Lexus and wriggle her hands into a pair of black driving gloves.

That night I dream of floors giving way to a black hole. I dream of explosions and shellfire from German sorties flying over the house and the amplified voice of the Wehrmacht: *"Achtung, Achtung!"* I dream of tree limbs falling down on my wife and baby, tree limbs that become quivering human limbs. I dream of giant Sunufu statues crashing down in a crumbling temple, blocking the exit as the ceiling caves in around my family. My father sails down the street in his sloop, wearing a double-breasted blue blazer and white pants. I call out for help but there's a tornado in my house, and the thunder and swirling wind carry my voice away.

"That's just going to look atrocious," I say.

"Walter, we're not going to have House Beautiful for a while," Sarah says, as one of Mitzy Baker's worker bees unscrews the retaining bolts of the wrought-iron banister from the stairs to replace it with a red inflatable hot-dog-shaped barricade.

"Caroline's barely moving yet."

Mitzy Baker glances at Sarah from the dining room, where she's cataloging and packing up our crystal and china, as if to say, Husbands, what can you do? She looks different today. I almost didn't recognize her without her hair band and blue pumps. She wears an old pair of paint-splattered jeans and a man's chamois-cloth shirt. Her face seems younger and friendlier as she goes to work with her hammer and screwdriver, installing latches, electrical tubing, lid locks on the toilets, outlet covers, elbow joints, gates, and foam rubber padding.

At lunchtime I leave work and drive home so I can check on the Baby Safe people. Not that I don't trust Sarah's judgment, it's just I know she's busy with the baby and might not be able to keep the necessary watchful eye on the workers.

I turn down Meadowbrook and see that the skateboarders are out in force. Nine twelve-year-old boys have skipped school and taken over the street for its smooth pavement, low curbs, and cars to challenge. I expect problems. But as I approach, a skinny kid with his hair cut high above his floppy ears, and floppy pants and big shoes to balance, has found a swell in the sidewalk that is perfect for lifting yourself up in the air, pulling your knees to your chest, falling off your board, and landing on your elbows. The street clears so I can pass scot-free.

I pull up in front of our house just as a couple of muscle guys in sweaty T-shirts are bringing out the ceiling fans, lugging them across the lawn and passing them up to a crew-cut sweaty guy in the back of a moving van. An old man in railroad-conductor overalls comes from around the back of the house carrying the Sunufu fertility statue, looking closely at its immense breasts and behind, wondering why it's considered art.

"Careful with that," I say. "That was used in actual ceremony." He looks at me as though I've spoken Swahili.

There's a blizzard of activity in the house. It takes me a minute to get my bearings. The first thing I notice is a college-age kid under the dining room table unscrewing the legs.

"Hey," I say. "The table's not going anywhere." He ducks his head out from under.

"I was told to pack the dining room," he says.

"No, no, no," I say, as the Moser chairs are moved out, two by two, by the crew-cut hit squad. "Put those down!" I say, "Put the chairs down; they're not going anywhere."

"We were told ten dining chairs to the truck," a thug with a scar on his head puffs. He produces a sheet of onionskin paper, which is covered with tomato stains from a meatball sub.

"Well, that's wrong," I say.

"You'll have to talk to Mitzy Baker about that," he says, going out the front door with the chairs, banging the legs on the doorframe.

I head upstairs, looking for Mitzy Baker, moving against the wall so a couple of men in blue coveralls can get by with my 27-inch TV, which Mitzy Baker said was wobbling on its stand. "Where's Mitzy Baker?" I ask.

"Haven't seen her, sir."

"How about my wife?"

"No, sir."

There's another college-age kid in my office yanking the nails out of my bookshelves, and through an open door I see a young woman in a gray hooded sweatshirt packing things from my darkroom. *No one* goes in my darkroom.

"Nope, not in here," I say, barreling across the room. "We're not touching any of this." I snatch a stack of stiff underdeveloped eight-by-tens I took of Sarah and Caroline in the woods near our house.

The woman looks up at me with her mouth open. The

young man starts to drag out a box of developing solutions. I grab hold of the other side.

"Hey, I just said this room doesn't get touched!"

"Talk to Mitzy Baker," he says, not even looking at me, yanking the box out of my grasp.

I rush downstairs. "Where's Mitzy Baker?" I ask four more sweaty crew-cut men who are carrying Sarah's great-grandmother's harpsichord down the front steps of the house.

"Backyard," one of the men huffs.

I tear around the house. Mitzy Baker is standing with two starch-haired helpers who are packing up our patio furniture. The three women are looking at our table umbrella and shaking their heads at our carelessness. The right gust of wind could lift the umbrella out of its stand and skewer the entire family on its pole.

Mitzy Baker peers up at me from her clipboard. "Hello, Mr. Peel." She smiles. "Sarah took Caroline to the park."

"They're packing my darkroom," I say. "Make them stop."

"All those chemicals," one of the women says.

"The heavy equipment," the other says.

Mitzy Baker closes her eyes. "Mr. Peel," she says. "The contract you signed specified that we remove any and all potential dangers from your house, and that includes your darkroom."

"Well, we can just forget that part of the contract."

"No, we can't, Mr. Peel. We do it all or nothing at all. Otherwise imagine the liability. We'd be out of business in a day."

"Fine. Nothing. You're out of here."

She closes her eyes again. She's said this to a thousand

clients before me. "You signed a legally enforceable contract, Mr. Peel, which provides severe remedies for breaches."

I stand out in front of our house and watch all my framed *New York Times* front pages being carried out to the truck: the day we landed on the moon, the day the Mets won the pennant, the day Nixon resigned. Then comes my darkroom: my enlarger, my dryer, boxes of solutions and tongs and timers, bags of undeveloped rolls of film I took of Caroline. I want to strangle everybody. But I'm late getting back to work. I head to the car.

The skateboarders have chosen our front wall as a new meeting place.

"Pardon me," I say. "Your skateboards are nicking our brickwork."

"Oh, sorry, sir," one of them says, the big one with premature facial hair cultivated into a Fu Manchu and goatee. He salutes, shoving his board under his arm like a rifle. "We'll never do it again. Sir!"

I turn to get in my car. I hear him say something behind my back, and the others begin to laugh.

"Have a nice day," he says.

"Good-bye," I say. Their girlfriends at the end of the wall giggle and light new cigarettes. I hope they're gone when Sarah and Caroline come back.

After work I drive up to the house and see Sarah and Mitzy Baker hugging on the front stoop. I keep driving. I wonder if my wife is having an affair with Mitzy Baker as I drive around the block. Then I realize how preposterous that is and pull up in front. My wife is crying, and Mitzy is holding her hands. I rush out of my car up the walk to Sarah and stand between her and Mitzy Baker. "Where's the baby?" I ask frantically.

"Inside," Sarah says. "The baby's fine."

"Then what is it?" Sarah sobs in my arms. "My God, what is it?" I look at Mitzy Baker, who's smiling her embroidered-kitten smile, her hands folded at her waist like a restaurant hostess.

"Mitzy thinks—" Sarah cries. "Mitzy says you should move out for a while." She stops crying. "Just until the house is done, Walter. It won't be for long. Just a few days."

I let go of my wife and straighten my back. "I'm not leaving." I'm unable to bear the sight of Mitzy Baker anymore. "This is my house."

"Mr. Peel," Mitzy Baker says, "you're paying Baby Safe four thousand dollars to make your house danger-free, yet you're standing in our way. Does that make any sense?"

"Caroline and I will come to see you every day, wherever you are," Sarah says.

"Forget it."

"Sarah and I are trying to come up with creative solutions, Mr. Peel. That's what motherhood is all about." Motherhood. That exclusive club. "Motherhood is about creativity." Mitzy Baker smiles as she crams me in with the rest of the worker ants who merely perform tasks and die early.

Caroline and I spend a few precious minutes together on the dining room floor while Sarah and Mitzy Baker stand outside talking. Mitzy Baker has said something to make Sarah laugh so hard she's holding her stomach, and Sarah's come back with something that causes Mitzy Baker to close her eyes and shake her head. The dining room smells like disinfectant and there's an echo. I notice the chandelier's gone. I look down and see Caroline crawling over to the liquor cabinet. I start to move toward her but stop myself. Let her go. She puts a little hand on the doorknob and rises up on her knees. Then she pulls on the door. The latch catches and the door locks with a loud click.

"Ha!" I say. "Gotcha!"

I'd stay in a hotel, but Baby Safe has made me so cash poor I have to ask my older brother to help me out for a few days. "Sure, Walt, *mi casa, su casa.*" Though it's not his casa at all. It belongs to Larissa, his twenty-two-year-old girlfriend, which is how my brother has managed to live since graduating from college twenty years ago. "She doesn't know who Rap Brown is," he whispers proudly, as we watch her string beads on one of the macramé belts she sells at accessory conventions.

Peter has worn a black nylon and Velcro back brace around his middle ever since he threw his back out moving his stuff into Larissa's. But I think it doubles as a girdle, since his age has started to hit him in the gut. "I'll never have sex standing up again," he says, and he's not joking. I don't know what young girls see in older men, especially Peter. He's no provider. He snores. He's got skin flaps.

I sit on Larissa's couch and watch Peter's documentary about Chilean miners on a TV set that I can't help noticing is precariously balanced on an old Korean chest. Larissa brings me a wine cooler and sets it on a glass-top coffee table with sharp edges. Then she turns on a wobbly floor lamp and flips over a log in the fireplace with a pair of iron tongs. There are matches on low tables. There are house plants on the floor and hanging from the ceiling, their poisonous leaves shedding like fallout and no poison-control hotline number pasted to any of the phones. Cords hang from Levolor blinds on all the windows like nooses at a mass lynching. There are plastic cleaning bags hanging in open closets, pennies and beads spilled on the floor, bleach and dishwasher detergent on a low shelf by the kitchen sink. I ask Peter if all the pilot lights are lit on the stove.

"Yeah, I guess so," he says.

"The stove's electric," Larissa says.

"That's good," I say. "Electric stoves are good."

"I prefer gas," Larissa says.

"Shh," Peter says, and holds up a hand to quiet us while his image accuses the mine owner of exploiting his workers.

A noisy group of people walk by the door of the apartment. I notice there's only one dead-bolt lock. "A woman was held up at gunpoint right around the corner from where we live," I whisper to Larissa.

"Quiet," Peter snaps.

"Just two weeks after she'd moved out from the city to get away from all that," I continue. "A guy in a jogging suit. She didn't get a description of his face. She remembered the gun, though. Got a good description of the gun."

"Oh, my God," Larissa says.

"That's what happens in the suburbs," Peter says. "Suburbs are the most dangerous places in the world. Sarajevo's safer." He clicks the remote control with an angry jerk of his arm and the screen goes black.

"So," Larissa says, after a long silence. "How's the baby?"

"Fantastic," I say, and I'm not three minutes into all the incredible things Caroline does when I see Larissa's nostrils flare in a suppressed yawn.

"Well, you should really bring her over sometime," Larissa says.

"Love to," I say. Not in a million years, I think, noticing the paint peeling from a windowsill, the uncovered electrical outlets.

I spend the night in a canvas hammock listening to my brother snore and wheeze while Larissa hits him with a pillow to shut him up. They won't last. She'll grow tired of the snoring, the skin flaps, the moles, and the backaches.

I don't go to work the next day. My back hurts from the hammock. I haven't slept. I don't have my own shower or a good-morning kiss from my wife and a cuddle with my daughter. I'm thrown off-kilter. I call Sarah to come meet me in the park, but she says Mitzy Baker told her it was best not to see me while the house is being done. I eat a hot dog at ten in the morning and decide to go to work after all because there's no place else to go. My secretary has a stack of fifteen messages, but I don't call anyone or read anything or take any calls. I put my head down on the desk and wake up in time to have another hot dog for lunch in the park. I call Sarah to see if I can come home.

"Hang on," she says. She puts her hand over the receiver, and I can hear Mitzy Baker's sanctimonious voice muffled through the phone. "No, Walt, I'm sorry," Sarah says.

"But I'm not feeling well," I say. "I think I'm sick."

"Mitzy thinks you'll influence me."

"I want to see you, dammit," I say. "I want to see my daughter."

"Hang on," Sarah says. I hear more muffled discussion. "Okay, but just for a little while. We'll come to you."

We arrange to meet by the duck pond. I walk through the park. Four or five squad cars have driven over the grass and are scattered around at the top of the hill leading down to the creek, doors open, radios blaring static. Something bad's happened. The police are talking to a guy in jogging shorts and Nikes. He keeps wiping his forehead with a balled-up Kleenex. His lips are blue. He bends over and puts his hands on his knees. A cop brings a space blanket from the trunk of one of the cars and wraps it around the jogger's shoulders. He clasps the blanket at his neck. It covers him to the bottom of his shorts, so it looks like he's naked underneath. He's seen something horrible. It's always the joggers who find something bad. They've become our disaster scouts, the shock messengers of the metro page. Plainclothes cops are walking up the hill and going over. A crowd is forming. I don't want to know. I keep going. We moved here to get away from this sort of thing.

I stand by the duck pond waiting for our blue Volvo 850 station wagon to climb over the hill. When I see Sarah, I'm going to hold her so hard she'll push right through me. I'm going to swing my baby up in the air and twirl her around and kiss her until she's soaked with spit. Just when it feels like I've been waiting forever, Mitzy Baker's Lexus peeks over the top of the hill. I see my wife in the back next to Caroline, who's strapped in a car seat. Mitzy Baker drives up slowly next to me, her black-gloved hands clenching the wheel. She doesn't look at me; she keeps her squinted eyes on the road. Sarah puts her hands against the window. I put mine against hers on the other side. The car keeps rolling. I jog alongside. "Hi, honey," I say. I see Sarah mouth "Hi" through the sound-proof glass. "Hi, sweetheart!" I yell to Caroline, but she's occupied with a stuffed clown, a present from Mitzy Baker, and doesn't notice me. Sarah tries to get her attention as I try to open the door. It's locked. Caroline looks up at me but doesn't seem to recognize me. Sarah smiles sadly and shrugs. Mitzy Baker peels away and speeds off. I race after the car. Sarah is turned around in her seat with her hands against the back window. I tear after them. Mitzy Baker disappears around the corner with my family.

Larissa's sick of me. If she were in love with my brother she could possibly put up with my whining about not seeing my wife and baby and my chortling on and on about Caroline's first tooth and how I drove five miles an hour home from the hospital on the highway after she was born. "So I said to Sarah, 'Don't they know we have a baby in the car?' As everybody honked and passed me and flipped me the bird." Larissa smiles sweetly and sips her wine cooler, wondering when I'm leaving. Peter has fallen asleep on the couch.

In the morning I jump out of my hammock as excited as I was the day Caroline was born. I get to go home today! I go for a jog and shower and head into the office with renewed enthusiasm for my work. At three o'clock I give my secretary the rest of the day off and head home.

The skateboarders have rolled around the block to the

Mallorys, in search of a bigger, more difficult wall. Let them nick the Mallorys' brickwork for a while, I think, relieved they've moved on. There's a moving van outside the house where the woman was held up at gunpoint; two club chairs are being loaded into the back. I never even had the chance to introduce myself.

I turn onto my street. Something feels strange. It's hot here. It used to be noticeably cooler than the rest of town. No one's outside. The sun reflects off the hot pavement, the glare so strong I pull down my visor. All I can hear is a dog barking on the next block.

I pull up to my house, which I recognize now only by my neighbors' houses. Our trees are gone, our beautiful old beech trees with their umbrellas of leaves that kept us cool in summer and dry in the rain, where birds and squirrels lived. Pachysandra and ivy that once flowed down our hill to the street has been plucked out, ripped away. Our lawn looks sick and lonely, like a disastrous haircut. A couple of crows peck around at what's left of the yard. I almost expect to see blood on the tree stumps. I stand over the biggest stump—the one that used to be the tree that gave us leaf piles to jump in, shade in which to cool off, shelter from the rain, where I'd promised to hang a rope swing someday—and count the rings to see how old it was. I count sixty-three. Not old for a tree. It was in the prime of its life.

Then I'm hit with panic. I race to the front door. I need to get inside. But the door's been replaced with a solid titanium slab with five locks. I bang on it with my fist. The door's so thick it barely makes a sound. I feel my chest tighten. I'm going to die of a heart attack right here on my front stoop if I don't get in. I kick the door, throw my body against it. "Sarah! Sarah!" I press my ear to the door and listen. Nothing. I move over to look in the window, but all the windows have been plastered over. "Sarah!" I scream again. Then I hear the sound of a dead bolt turning. Then another. And another. Two more.

The door opens with massive reverberations and there is Sarah, holding the baby and peeking out from behind the door. "Walter!" she cries.

I push open the door and step inside. Sarah's wearing a stained terry robe, which is open, and she's naked underneath. The baby's wearing only a diaper. Sarah puts her free hand to her mouth and starts to cry. I wrap my arms around them both.

"Walter, I was so scared," she says, in a little whimper. "I thought someone was trying to break in."

"It's okay, it's me." I hold them tighter. "Everything is fine."

"They took the trees."

"Shhh." I look around our house, which is empty except for a few large soft toys. The windows are now continuations of the walls, the fireplace is boarded up, the furniture is gone. The banister and staircase have been replaced with an impassable barrier, and why not? There's no need for an upstairs anymore. I'm sure there's no bed for the baby to fall off, no shower or bath for the baby to drown in. Our house looks more like a cave than an English-style cottage. This is, in fact, how cave people lived: two people who mate for life taking care of, and protecting, one baby. That's why our species has survived so well.

The three of us sit on the cushy floor, covered with Mitzy Baker's foam padding. Sarah chose toffee, which makes the place dark but cozy. It's a nice product, just as Mitzy Baker said. Caroline can drag herself up on her toys and fall and not feel a thing.

I pull my wife and child into me as hard as I can and feel the need and ache of togetherness, the relief of being inside. Tomorrow we can wake up and relax, finally. Tonight we can sleep without dreaming.

Dentaphilia

I once loved a woman who grew teeth all over her body.

The first one came in as a hard spot in her navel. It grew quickly into a tooth, a real tooth with a jagged edge and a crown, enameled like a pearl. I thought it was sexy, a little jewel in her belly button. Helen would bunch up her shirt, undulate like a harem dancer, and I'd be ready to go.

Then one day I came home from the mill and Helen called for me to come upstairs. She sat at the foot of our bed wrapped in a towel, still wet and shiny from the shower. She lifted her arm. I felt around. With her arm raised I could make out the outline of a row of upper incisors pressing out just under her skin. My God, I thought, the soft underside of her arm would soon resemble a crocodile's jaw. She said it'd been itching and painful there for some time. I told her not to worry. It was nothing. It would go away. I even managed to make her believe me long enough for her to go to sleep and for me to lie awake all night wondering what the hell to do. But in the morning, when she scratched my thigh with a molar that had sprouted in the crease behind her knee, I called Dr. Manfred.

"Yes, well . . . yes, well . . ." Dr. Manfred murmured as he examined Helen's body with a small magnifying glass that looked like the kind jewelers use to appraise diamonds. With each "yes, well" my chest expanded, tightening my shirt at the buttons. I thought my ribs would burst out of my shirt and pile up on the floor like sticks.

"Well, what?" I asked.

He drew the glass away from his eye and smiled a phony smile. "I can see how you thought they were teeth."

He produced a little scalpel from his white coat and began to scrape away at one of the teeth on the inside of Helen's elbow. It came off in thin translucent strips like the layers of an onion. Helen squeezed her lips together but didn't complain. She was brave when it came to pain. In a metal bowl, he ground the tooth with a marble pestle into a fine white powder like sand.

"You have calcinosis, my dear," Dr. Manfred said. "It's a calcification condition." He pushed up on a turquoise soap dispenser and rubbed his hands into a fat lather cloud. "Sometimes there's a buildup of calcium deposits in the body," he said, over running tap water. "We don't normally see the calcification externally, perhaps a plaque in the dermis, a deposit in the nodule. Not a worry, though." He shook his hands dry in the air. "We'll run some blood, check the thyroid. These things usually just go away. *Poof!*"

Helen pinched the sand in the metal bowl between her thumb and index finger, rubbed some into her palm, let it run through her fingers back into the bowl. Dr. Manfred wrote a prescription for a calcium substitute and told her to lay off salt.

In the morning Helen rolled over and I saw a long series of evenly spaced holes in the sheet, as if boll weevils had been eating the bed. By scraping off the tooth on her elbow, Dr. Manfred had just made room for more. Helen had teeth sticking out all the way up her arm. Her shoulder looked like the back of a stegosaurus. A fool could have told me that Dr. Manfred was the wrong kind of doctor.

Dr. Freedman's waiting room had little chairs and little tables with crayons and coloring books. Some kid had already rifled through and scribbled everything green. Green duck, green cow, green Bo-Peep, green sheep.

"The dentist sees grown-ups too?" I asked the receptionist.

"Yes, grown-ups too," she assured me, in a little voice.

I gave Helen the last grown-up chair and sat in one of the little ones. My knees came to my head. The kid at my table was really upset about all the coloring books being colored in, and his mother was telling him to try drawing his own pictures from his imagination. He looked at her like she was stupid. Then he noticed Helen. All the kids were looking at her with their mouths open, even when their mothers told them it wasn't polite. Even when Helen smiled at them and said hello, they couldn't stop gaping. The row of lower bicuspids coming in across her cheekbone was too much.

She was in Dr. Freedman's office for an hour. I started pacing. Then two hours. The other patients were agitated, and the receptionist was making apologies on the dentist's behalf. "I'm sure it's an urgent matter," she said. "You'll want him to give you the time *you* need when it's your turn."

"What took so long?" I asked, driving home.

"I have hyperstimulated dentin," she said, looking out her window at the shadows from the trees. "He wants me to stop taking the calcium substitute. And he wants to see me in a week."

"What for?"

"He says I have twelve cavities." She flipped down the cosmetic mirror on the visor and freshened her lipstick.

"Leave this to me, Hel," I said. "You concentrate on getting well, and leave the rest to me." I reached over and touched her knee.

She turned toward me. "Can you pull over? I need to walk."

"Whatever you want," I said, stopping the truck on the shoulder.

"I'll see you at home." She climbed down.

"I'll come too," I said.

"I need to be alone for a while," she said, and closed the door.

Dentaphilia

` ` `

The teeth started coming in pretty regularly. Every morning there'd be something new to report, something pressing against the skin, a toughening between her toes, a hard place on her ear. Then a few days would go by with nothing, and I'd think maybe the whole business was going to go away, as Dr. Manfred said. But soon the cramp Helen had been rubbing on her hip would explain itself with a freshly cut tooth or a red spot above her eyebrow would open up to a molar.

"Just how ugly am I, Mike?" she asked one morning, staring out front at some squirrels that were draining the seeds from her bird feeders.

I moved her hair away and looked at her face, which was blotched and speckled with incisors. "You could never be ugly, Hel," I said. And I meant it.

I spent a lot of spare time chopping and stacking wood in the back, trying to figure out how to keep Helen from being scared, thinking about how much I loved her and how going through this experience together *confirmed* to me how much I loved her.

One afternoon I heard her singing in the downstairs bathroom: "Delta Dawn," to be precise. I leaned my ax against the stump and moved over to where I could see her, in front of the medicine chest mirror, rubbing the teeth on her body with peroxide and a chamois cloth like they were little pieces of carved crystal. She had her hair twisted into a new do with a sunflower barrette and shimmery pink gloss on her lips. She'd bought a new dress, a yellow gabardine that pinched in under her breasts, fit tightly at her waist, and buttoned all the way down. I watched her put on earrings, little zircons that picked up the light, and hook a matching necklace behind her neck. Then she looked over and saw me standing there with my hands against the window, my breath fogging up the glass, and screamed bloody murder.

Helen was at Dr. Freedman's office every other day for this or that. "He says I need another cleaning," she'd say, or, "He wants more X rays." I'd sit in that kids' waiting room for hours, listening to Helen giggle and squeal in the office. Once, when things got too quiet, I went in. I found her giddy and stupid on nitrous.

"You can't expect her to get treatment with no anesthesia," Dr. Freedman said, snapping off latex gloves. Helen pulled one out of his hand, blew it up into a five-fingered balloon, and let it zip across the room. I pulled her out of the office by her wrist.

In the truck, Helen was furious. She said I was way out of line. I tried arguing with her but she told me not to bother her, she was cutting a tooth on her neck, out of that place just above the spine where, without thinking, I used to reach over and put my fingers on long trips or in traffic.

I came home from the mill one night and Helen had left a note saying to go ahead and eat without her. I made a sandwich with a couple of slices of cheese that had hardened around the edges and about half a cup of mayonnaise to mask the taste of some old turkey. Then I watched beach volleyball on ESPN.

Helen was undressing when I woke up. Naked, she was a treasure from King Tut's tomb, a gilded statue covered in jewels. For one sleepy moment I thought she was the most beautiful thing I'd ever seen. Then I realized what I was looking at. "Are you insane?" I asked, about her rows upon rows of gold fillings. "We can't afford those. What were you thinking?"

"They were a gift from Dr. Freedman."

That put me over the top. I wasn't going to lose the woman I loved to a dentist. I pulled on my pants, threw on a shirt and shoes, and grabbed Helen by the wrist.

"I thought you'd like them," she cried, as I yanked her bathrobe off a nail on the door and dragged her from the house. "I did them for you!"

I forced her into the truck and peeled out of the driveway. With Helen screaming and grabbing onto the strap above the window, I swerved and cut corners, thirty miles over the speed limit.

Dr. Freedman lived in a new brick split-level connected to his office. He opened his huge front door when I rapped the gaudy lion-head knocker. He was in pajamas: blue silk. Helen was trying to wiggle out of my grip and kicking me in the shins with her sharp little feet.

"Why don't you come in, Mike. We'll talk it over." Freedman was trying to sound as if he were the one in control and I was the crackbrain.

"We don't want any of your handouts!" I yelled.

"They were a gift, Mike. Professional courtesy. For all the business Helen's brought."

"Take 'em out."

"That's not reasonable, Mike. You're not being reasonable." Freedman held his skinny little hands up, his only defense, as I moved toward him to bust his mouth in. Helen was screaming. I was hurting her wrist. I let her go and she ran across the lawn. The dentist and I just stood there like a couple of lazy dogs and watched her run, her feet cutting divots into the dentist's lawn, her teeth opalescent in the moonlight.

I didn't go to work the next day. I couldn't get out of bed. I called the mill and said I had the flu. I called all of Helen's girlfriends to see if they'd seen her. Around noon I drove around to places Helen liked to go—Hatcher's Boutique, Sweet Nothings, Flower Emporium—knowing full well she wouldn't be seen in any of those places now. I bought some roses at the Emporium, came home, and watched TV. Five o'clock that afternoon Helen came in. She'd had the gold replaced with porcelain. She thanked me for the flowers and went upstairs for a bath. I stood outside the bathroom door and asked her if she wanted a glass of wine, cocoa, warm towels from the dryer, a sandwich, some music, an inflatable pillow for her neck, anything. No, thank you. No, thank you, nothing.

"If you want to do something," she called, when I ran out of offers and started to move away from the door, "you can wash my back."

I pushed open the door. She sat with her arms resting on the sides of the lion-claw tub like a queen. I lowered myself to my knees. She opened her mouth a little and I kissed her. She didn't kiss me back but she didn't push me away either. I dragged my tongue down her neck and around a circle of pointed teeth that surrounded her nipple like a fortress. She raised her chest. Then I scooped the soap out of the dish and rubbed up a lather. She bent forward, causing little murky waves to lap at the sides of the tub. The water was filled with lumps of chalky powder. I looked up at the ceiling to see if the plaster had come loose. Then I looked at her back. The skin was peeling as if she'd had a bad sunburn, rolling up and coming off in shavings.

"I know what it looks like," Helen said, before I could say anything. "Wash along the edges. It'll help it along."

"Help it along to what?" I managed to ask. Underneath the old skin she was tender, wrinkled and pink like a newborn. I was afraid to touch, worried I'd hurt her. She said it didn't hurt, it just itched and stung a bit. Then I saw a couple of teeth bob to the surface of the bathwater like a row of miniature buoys on a dark and rocky bay.

For a little while it seemed like everything was getting back to normal. Every morning we'd find a few more teeth somewhere in the bed or swirling around in the shower drain. Throw them out, get rid of them, I said, but Helen saved them in a little Zulu basket. "For jewelry," she said, holding them in her hands like precious stones. "Maybe a necklace." I was so happy and giddy during that time, she could have worn the basket on her head and I wouldn't have objected. I bought her things. I took her dancing even though I'm no dancer.

Freedman cautioned otherwise. "Helen needs special care during this period," he said. "She's completely defenseless." He'd called me into his office to talk about her recent blood test. There was an excess of calcium carbonate in her blood. He was concerned about the shedding.

"You're looking at me like you think I can't take care of my wife," I said.

Freedman shrugged. I knew he was in love with her. I mean, everybody was in love with Helen. I used to sit on a stool at the Mug, where she bartended, drinking diluted whiskey, waiting for a chance to talk to her. Two other guys did the same. But it was my car she slid into after work one snowy night, my lap she swung her leg over, and my hand that slid the ponytail holder out of her long brown hair. Now she was getting better. She wasn't going to need him anymore. He was losing her and couldn't bear it.

More of the teeth dropped out and the skin on her back healed and in time the calcium in her blood dropped way down.

But then things started to get bad again.

One beautiful spring morning I came out of the mill and Helen was sitting on the hood of our truck, kicking her heels against the tire like a little girl. "My wisdom teeth are coming in." She smiled proudly.

I froze. "Where?"

She lowered her eyes bashfully and raised them. "Down there."

"Oh," I said. What are you supposed to say when your wife tells you something like that? "Oh."

She put her arms around my neck and slipped her butt off the hood. She felt like a wisp of grass. Then my brain bucked into action and I realized she was falling. And I was dropping her. I caught her under her arms before she broke on the asphalt.

"I'm fine, Mike. Really fine. Just a little wobbly." She moved away from me and did little herky-jerky pirouettes around the parking lot, like a glass ballerina on top of a busted music box.

To say the teeth started coming back in would be an understatement. They knocked down doors and *busted* back in. They grew in mounds on top of one another, in notched clumps like fallen stones from a temple ruin, in clusters like tiled mosaics. They grew straight and crooked and upside down and ingrown. You could sit and watch them grow, see them force their way out. Helen said it didn't hurt. She even got excited when she felt one coming. "Look at that one," she'd squeal. "Oh! Here comes another!" And she'd brush and rub them with baking soda and peroxide, spend all day in front of the mirror singing and polishing.

Helen wasn't in Freedman's office fifteen minutes when I lost patience and barged in. He looked at me as if he were really tired of my intrusions. Well, too bad for you, I thought. When I came around the chair I saw he had her legs in stirrups. "They're impacted," he said.

The whole business with Dr. Freedman had made me crazy. They were always talking on the phone and laughing and having appointments every day. In my mind, I saw them together, passing the rubber tube of the nitrous tank back and forth. I saw her legs hung over the arms of the chair with Freedman crouched down at the yummy end of things. "Hope you don't mind the drill," he'd say, and think he was so funny because she'd laugh and wrap her arms around his neck, pulling him up into her.

I started following her, listening in to her phone calls on the other line. But I was a bad spy. I kept getting caught. "I know you're there, Mike," she'd say on the phone, talking to one of her girlfriends about a beauty makeover in a magazine. "I hear you breathing." And I'd hang up and sit on my hands on the bed. Once she tapped on my car window in the parking lot of the Price Chopper, where I'd fallen asleep watching her shop. "Relationships have to be based on trust, Mike," she yelled through the glass, "or there's *no* relationship." She was getting nasty. She snapped at me all the time. I couldn't do anything right.

One night she stormed out of the house on the crutches she had to use now that her legs had gone so stiff. She said she and Dr. Freedman were going to the symphony.

"The symphony?" I said, from the front stoop.

"Yes," she hissed back. "The symphony."

"What for?" I said.

"For culture," she growled, right up in my face, three little canines on the end of her pointed chin. "You and me, Mike, we have no culture."

That was the night I tried to be with another woman. Robin was a waitress at the Mug who always wanted to get together with me when I only wanted Helen. We went back to her apartment, but I didn't like touching her. She felt too soft and squishy. I missed Helen's rough spots, her premolars and molars, her pointy canines and wisdoms, the soft areas next to the hard areas. I missed being inside Helen and the challenge of going around the sharp places. Robin felt like Silly Putty, like I could stretch and bend her and tie her up with herself.

I apologized to Robin and got up to go. When we were putting our clothes back on, she said there were doctors who could help me with my problem. She said this in a mean way, not in a helpful way.

Helen was in bed when I got home, the sheet pushed down to her waist. In the cool streetlight that shone through the window, I could see the phosphorescent glow of the thick clumps of teeth that stuck all over her back like barnacles. I shucked off my clothes and slid in next to her. We slept on satin sheets, not because they're sexy but because satin was the only material that didn't catch on the teeth that covered most of her body now. She perched herself up on her elbows and waited for me to talk.

"I want things back the way they were," I said. "I miss us."

In the morning we went to Dr. Freedman's and Helen told him to pull the teeth. All of them. I expected him to tell me I was a hateful son-of-a-bitch, but he nodded professionally and spread out his tools. He offered gas, Novocain, a sedative. Helen waved him off. He started with the molars on her rib cage. He used tweezers to pluck out the little teeth on her face and pliers for the bigger molars across her collarbone. He yanked, twisted, and pulled and went on to the next. But something bad oozed out of those holes where the teeth had been, not the red blood that inevitably flows after a pulled tooth. This blood was black-red, the kind of blood that comes from deep inside you and doesn't want to be disturbed. Helen let out a low, sorrowful moan.

"Stop," I said finally. "No more."

I took her to the beach. She wanted to smell the salt and feel the air, let the sounds of gulls and waves lull her to sleep. By now her beautiful face was covered in teeth. I wrapped her in a satin quilt and put oven mitts on her hands, which had become rough and bent. I laid her brittle body against a dune, and we stayed there together like that for three days.

She said she was sorry time ran out on us and she wished we'd had kids. She apologized for going to the symphony with Dr. Freedman. "He made me feel pretty," she said. "I know it was wrong."

"I always thought you were beautiful," I said. "I still do."

After the second day she couldn't talk anymore because her tongue had calcified. I told her stories. I made them up out of nowhere. There was the giant turnip that crushed a big city, the eyeballs that took over the world. Her favorite was the talking stadium that fell in love with a cheerleader, got his heart broken, and then realized—too late, because he'd already caved in and killed everybody—that his real love was the hot-dog lady in one of his concession stands who had been there all along inside him.

On the third day I woke up at sunrise and saw her looking up at pelicans flying in formation over the dunes. I'd seen pelicans in the Outer Banks of North Carolina, but never this far north. They flew southeast and faded away. Helen was still looking up.

"Whatcha lookin' at, Hel?" I looked where she was looking. But there was nothing up there. Not even a cloud.

Now and then I stumble on an oasis, palm trees, blue water, and there's Helen leaning on a tree in the yellow dress she was buried in and yellow shoes, holding a banana daiquiri she made for me. I take a drink of the daiquiri, but the cold hits my brain and gives me a headache. She says, "Poor baby, let me rub it," and holds out smooth ivory hands. Then she slips through my arms. Dissolves into sand. I grab at her, but the more I grab, the more sand caves in around me, and it's not until I'm buried to the waist that I realize she's gone.

The Woman Who Cut Off Her
Leg at the Maidstone Club

Word spread down East Beach that a woman had cut off her foot in front of the Maidstone Club.

None of the club members budged from their chaises or stepped out from under their candy-striped umbrellas. They assumed that the woman was a day visitor who'd ridden in on the back of a motorcycle or a renter who'd wandered over, burnt and bewildered, from West Beach. But then, to their astonishment, word spread that the woman was Maisie Haselkorn of the Eastport Haselkorns. With that dispatch, the entire East Beach population migrated toward Maidstone, nonchalantly, so as not to appear too impressed.

But the news was wrong. She hadn't severed her foot. Not yet. Rather, using a penknife, she'd carved a broken line into the skin below the left ankle, like a doctor preparing for surgery, and tied an Hermès scarf around her calf as a tourniquet. The foot was buried under a mosaic of mosquito bites, which Maisie'd rubbed raw with sand and salt water, unable to stop the violent itching. A low wolverine growl came from Maisie's throat as, teeth bared, nails worn to nubs, she gouged at one bite, her eyes already moving on to the next. Athletic and limber, Maisie raised her foot to her mouth and gnawed off the tops of the bites that lined her soft instep.

"Grammy used to mix vinegar and baking soda," an August renter offered.

"Scratch off the top of 'em, then pour on a jigger of Rebel Yell," a day visitor in puka-shell jewelry advised. "Burns like four-alarm chili, but those sons-a-bitches get what they deserve."

"Leonine amusement," Pasty Plugh scoffed to Skimpy Pimscott, struggling for a look over the crowd of day visitors and renters with their zinc-covered noses and coconut stench. "August in East has become unbearable."

"Yes, but poor Maisie," Skimpy whispered. Pasty stood on tiptoes, then elbowed her way through. When she saw the foot, covered in a mountain range of bloody red bites, she brought her hands to her mouth and gasped.

Club members did not get mosquito bites. The skin and blood of families like the Plughs, the Pimscotts, the Haselkorns, and the Trums didn't appeal to the local insect life. Instead they fed on the imported flesh of renters like the Newmans, the Nathans, the Fussellis, and the Golds. Or the leather of day visitors like—does it matter? But Maisie Haselkorn, daughter of Electra von Hardweger Haselkorn

and the late F. Whitmire "Fuzzy" Haselkorn, was so infused
with the bodily fluids of Ben Loeb, the West Beach land developer, that her genetic resistance to bugs had been dulled.
And now they swarmed around her, hovered overhead, le-
gions of mosquitoes probing her with their bloodsucking pro-
boscises.

"I knew it would lead to a bad end," Skimpy told Mim
Trum.

"Isn't there something I can do?" Pasty Plugh asked
Maisie, swatting the insects away with her hand.

"Oh, no, Pasty," Maisie said, scratching and gnawing and
slapping. "It's just that the itching is so . . . annoying."

Scraping her foot with the sharp edge of a broken
clamshell and oblivious of the crowd, Maisie looked out over
the Sound toward Haselkorn Island, a place she'd never
been, where, all morning, ferries had delivered land-moving
equipment to break ground for the new condominiums, hotels, and restaurants. From here it was only a dollop of green
in an aluminum sea.

Ben Loeb slapped a mosquito on his arm and followed Maisie
Haselkorn out of Mim Trum's dinner honoring Lizzy Mann,
who'd sung a benefit for children with AIDS at East Town
Hall. She'd been just out of his grasp at all the parties that
season, but tonight she'd asked him to hold her drink while
she showed Chrispo Pimscott how to use the indoor rubber-
ized rock climber. Ben had to jog to keep up with Maisie's
stride.

"Mim's going to ask Lizzy to sing," Ben said.

"I don't like entertainment at parties." Maisie swung her

arms with clenched fists. "And I have no interest in hearing Lizzie Mann sing."

Ben looked at this graceful woman in the cool moonlight. She was tallish and thin with the skin and nose of good breeding. Hers were the choice chromosomes, encoded with healthy hair, good nails, straight teeth, and athletic ability. She'd been star pentathlete at Grangerville. Her Grangerville yearbook, "The Golden Nut," captured her personality and athletic prowess in a photograph mid-hurdle with a caption that read, "She throws, she jumps, that winning attitude— MAISIE!"

"I'm Ben Loeb. I met you at the Clayborns' dinner for that artist."

"Ramsey Angus Hunter. I didn't like him *or* his guillotine imagery. And I know who you are, Mr. Loeb."

"Call me Ben."

"You built the new strip mall in North East."

"We prefer 'convenience center.' The industry considers Loeb Commons to be architecturally significant." He thought she'd be impressed.

"I like the older buildings, myself," Maisie said. "I don't like all those implied lines and oddly shaped rooms. And I don't like new architecture that tries to look like old architecture."

"Why don't we just stop all building altogether?" He was becoming aroused by this young woman, so fiercely certain of her opinions.

"Yes, why don't we."

Ben was getting winded. "Why don't you have a car like everyone else?"

"I do," she said. "I told him to leave. And what about you, Mr. Loeb? Where's your car?"

"I'll get it in the morning," Ben said. Maisie looked at him, perplexed. Ben noticed one of her eyes was higher on her face than the other. "I'm spending the night with you."

"Don't think I don't know what you're after, Mr. Loeb." Maisie leaned back luxuriously on a pale-chintz fainting couch.

Ben lifted his head from between her thighs. "Please, call me Ben."

"You want Haselkorn Island," she said. "But you're wasting your time with me. I'm an Eastport Haselkorn, not an Island Haselkorn. The Eastport Haselkorns split from the Island Haselkorns in 1650, and the two sides haven't spoken since. You'll have to build your hotels and condominiums elsewhere."

Haselkorn Island. Four square miles of undeveloped land. The island had been part of a royal grant over three hundred years ago. The sight of it made Ben drool like an infant. Word had it the heirless and ancient Lord Cotton Haselkorn of the Island Haselkorns was considering its disposition.

"Make me ambassador of goodwill." Ben moved Maisie's knees farther apart with his chin. "It's time you kissed and made up."

He was the hairiest man Maisie'd ever seen. When she first saw him undressed, that night after Mim Trum's party, she childishly squeezed her eyes shut, wishing the hair would go away when she opened them. But now that she knew every inch of him, she loved every hair. She loved the way it was so long in places it curled, how when he walked out of the ocean it matted down slick like a seal, how when he was cold it stood out from his body like quills on a porcupine. The men she'd been accustomed to before Ben—Carlsbad Trum, Rennie Pimscott, Minty Serk, well-born men with smooth, hairless chests and backs—seemed childlike now, underdeveloped. Next to Ben, those hairless attractions seemed pedophilic.

Electra Haselkorn kept a sharp eye on her daughter and the West Beach developer who came as Maisie's date to all the parties now, suspicious of the intentions of a newcomer. "All that hair, Maisie," she said, watching Ben jackknife into the Esterhouses' pool. "It suggests a questionable background." But seeing the telltale insect bites on Maisie's ankles, and the bottles of calamine, Bactine, Off!, and other foul-smelling potions Maisie kept hidden in her closets, Electra knew it was too late. The Ben Loeb virus would have to run its course. She knew from her own love affair thirty-two years earlier with Joey Ottominelli, the contractor Luciano Ottominelli's son, that love, true love, enters the blood like barbiturate, and once you've had it you can't do without. Watching Maisie bend to scratch a welt behind her knee, just as she herself had scratched thirty-two years before, Electra knew Ben Loeb was all through her daughter like an infection.

Denied their petition to enjoin office-furniture king Al Rodman and his wife, Carol, from building an oceanfront temple substantially resembling the Pan Am terminal at Kennedy, Skimpy and Chrispo Pimscott decided to throw the royal couple a Bastille Day party.

On the day of the event, Maisie leaned back dreamily against the Pimscotts' superior weeping English beech—a majestic pendulous-branched tree for which the office-furniture king had offered $80,000 for the rights to uproot and replant on his own property, an increasingly common practice of the island's newcomers to transform *terra nova* to *terra antiqua*. Chrispo had refused the gruesome tender and would not even entertain sponsoring the arriviste's membership at Maidstone.

When Maisie opened her eyes, Ben was ducking under the tree's thick leafy canopy. He took her arm and led her up to the Pimscotts' roof, where he made love to her as guests arrived below. Maisie planted her feet against two window cornices to brace herself.

"Darling, would you like me to take the slate?" Ben offered.

Maisie considered his kind proposal to be on the bottom, then decided it was better to have a scraped back than an exposed backside. Just as Ben had promised, no one looked up—except the driver of one of the catering trucks. And when one of Maisie's sandals slipped off the roof and hit Lord Cotton Haselkorn's man Nils on the shoulder as he was rolling the lord's wheelchair up a makeshift ramp to the Pimscotts', Nils gently tucked the shoe into the veteran turtle-shaped boxwood by the entrance.

"Maisie, your back," Electra Haselkorn said, of the slate indentations pressed into her daughter's skin.

"Those awful new chaises at Maidstone, Mother."

"I'll talk to Gerard first thing tomorrow," Electra said.

"Do that, Mother." Maisie crossed the room to say hello to Mim Trum. Electra noticed she was missing a shoe.

As the first course was cleared and the main course was served, Ben manipulated Maisie under the table with his foot while carrying on a discussion with Pasty Plugh about the challenge of fishing for fluke.

"I never have any luck fluking," Pasty said breezily.

"There's a trick," Ben said. Maisie pressed down on his big toe.

"A trick?" Pasty puckered her forehead.

"A secret," Ben said.

"A secret!" Pasty flushed ruby, as though it were her own pants being moved aside by the toes of a hairy land developer. Ben moved in close to Pasty's ear, his salmon-Wellington breath hot on her neck.

"Let the sinker bounce on the bottom." His breathy voice sent an electric shock down Pasty's viscera.

"Isn't that fascinating." Pasty's voice quivered. "Pinky," she said in a loud whisper to Mr. Plugh, swallowing his fifth Glenlivet at a nearby table. "Pinky," she called again through closed teeth.

Pinky Plugh, red-faced and spider-veined, had heard his wife the first time and hoped his selective deafness would make her retreat.

"Pinky!" The room went quiet.

"Yes, Pasty," Pinky said, with resignation, as though Mrs. Plugh's summons were the last torment he could bear.

"Mr. Stein here says—"

"That's Loeb, actually," Ben interrupted.

"Mr. Loeb here says to let the sinker bounce on the bottom." The room became quiet enough to hear the gentle popping of Ben's toe joint. And then, one by one, at each table throughout the grand dining room, living room, and side parlor, they began to consider Ben's fluking technique.

"Let the sinker bounce on the bottom. . . ."

"The sinker . . ."

". . . bounce on the bottom."

"Of course!"

"It fools the fluke, you see."

"We'll take out the *Ebb Tide* tomorrow. . . ."

". . . charter the *Catch as Catch Cannes* tomorrow. . . ."

Pinky slammed his fist on his table. "Nonsense," he bellowed. *"Pre*-posterous!" Again the guests became quiet. Pinky Plugh wasn't going to listen to the nouveau fishing advice of a West Beacher. Certainly not one whose beard was merely a continuation of his chest hair. "Next you'll be proselytizing plastic bait and treble hooks. Why not just dredge the Sound?"

Battle lines were drawn throughout the party, with Pinky and Pasty as opposing generals.

"I'll have you know, young man"—Pinky pointed at Ben—"that I was Fluke Champion, 1962, Newport Beach."

"Oh, shut up, Pinky," Pasty said.

As the crowd one by one joined forces with Pinky and bore down on Ben, Lord Cotton Haselkorn, the last of the Island Haselkorns, had his man Nils roll him to Ben's table. Most East Beachers were too young to remember that Lord

Haselkorn was Champion Bottom Fisher for 1926, '27, and '32, back when the Sound was filled with flounder, fluke, and sweet sole, long before regulation lengths and Fish & Game wardens.

"I fluked the same way." Lord Haselkorn smiled toothlessly.

"I know," Ben said. "I read an interview in the *East Ledger.*"

"My boy, that was sixty years ago."

So taken was Lord Haselkorn with Ben that he invited him aboard the *Hi C's* for an inshore fishing tour around Haselkorn Island. So impressed would the lord be by Ben's trolling technique, and engaged by Ben's stories of birding in Gabon and womanizing among the Yanomami Indians in Brazil, that by the time the sun would drop behind West Beach, Lord Haselkorn would bequeath his island and all of its treasures to Ben Loeb.

But now the crowd was closing in on Ben. "Save the fluke!"

"Save the Sound!"

"If those West Beach developers have their way," Matilda Serk shouted, "they'll landfill the entire Sound for more condominiums and hotels!"

Then came a climaxing groan from Maisie—not a feminine sigh of ecstasy but the sorrowful moan of a woman who knows she's not needed anymore, desired anymore, knows she will never be made love to this way again. It is a cry that cannot be mistaken for anything other than the death song of a woman who knows the end of the greatest love affair of her life. The shouting in the rooms died to a drone that seemed to mirror Maisie's cry. It was a cry that Pasty Plugh knew so well that she clasped her throat with her hands and felt she would choke from the lump gathering there. The Countess Loretta Mach, in white tulle and the Mach jewels, recognized that cry from the night she gave up Robért, her Corsican lover, for this life of parties, pools, Fabergé, and furniture. Mim Trum covered her face and wept for Tony Donatucci, and Skimpy called out for Shecky Moskowitz.

"So it's a date?" Lord Haselkorn held out a gnarled hand.

"It's a date," Ben said, and slipped his busy toe and foot back into his Top-Sider.

Carlsbad Trum, crow-faced and cadaverous, drove a ball so far off the links at Maidstone he'd been wandering the beach a half hour. Searching here and there, using his hand as a visor, resting his driver on his shoulder, he spotted the ball rolling to and fro at the water's edge. "Worse than I feared," he said. "Talk about hitting into the rough." Carlsbad noticed Maisie as he bent to pick up his ball, which the tide took out of reach. "Hello, Maisie, cutting off your foot, I see."

Maisie was sawing through her slender talus with a penknife from Cartier. The crowd had long since dispersed: the renters, tired of waiting for her to finish the job, went back to their cottages; the day visitors rode back to wherever they came from; the club members rushed home to scratch the Eastport Haselkorns off their guest lists.

Carlsbad peered over Maisie's athletic shoulders, rocked up onto his toes, and tried to look down her thin cotton top. Then, seeing that Maisie was not in a talkative mood, he

scooped up his ball as the tide brought it in and trudged back
over the sand to the links.

It was late in the day when Maisie balanced herself like a gym-
nast and flipped her left leg into the ocean. "Why stop at the
foot?" she'd said, slicing into the deep fascia of her tan thigh.
The leg skipped across the surface and tumbled into a beach
break. The Pimscotts' golden, Pal, small-brained but fiercely
loyal, did what any champion retriever would do. He sprang
from the hole he'd been digging all afternoon and dove into
the surf to fetch.

"Oh, Pal," Maisie said, disgusted, as the immaculate pedi-
gree dropped the leg and jumped deliriously in anticipation
of his next fetch, "you overbred idiot." Pal chased his tail and
shook his long wet fur.

Remember all your strength from pentathlon, Maisie
thought. On her remaining leg, she hopped around in a circle; faster and faster, pirouetting, swinging the leg by the toes,
she flung it to the sea. Way beyond the break the leg flew, end
over end, foot over thigh. Even the idiot dog, Pal, knew it was
outside his range. And now Maisie, free of itching at last, fell
in the sand, craned her neck back, and looked into the mango
sun that was sinking upside down behind Maidstone. "That's
better," she sighed, wiggling her fresh stump. "That's much
better."

Covered

My mother said that as a boy I was never without my old blanket: I slept with it, ate with it, and dragged it along behind me like an animal on a leash.

That was our last coherent conversation. Soon after, she became anxious and confused, at times mistaking me for my dead father and then not recognizing me at all. One of those nights I came home from the hospital and climbed the back steps to the attic. I hadn't been up there since I'd moved home to care for my parents. Under a wardrobe rack filled with dresses, a fox stole, and my mother's wedding gown, I found the box marked STEVEN'S STUFF.

The packing tape fought me all the way, the old glue stringy, like gauze being pulled off a wound. Inside were my baseball trophies, a handprint of a seven-year-old boy set in plaster unevenly painted green, my President's Fitness Award, a folder of report cards. And there at the bottom was my blanket, used as padding for lopsided pottery and my great ceramic opus: a clay animal chess set, felines and canines with smashed faces and broken tails.

I lifted it out, the other objects collapsing together, and held it in my hands. I fingered the material and brought it to my face. I could isolate smells: attic must was predominant, but then honeysuckle (my mother's perfume), Shalimar (my grandmother's), catalpa, urine, and sweat. I rubbed the material some more between my fingers, got the old rhythm going, felt the ancient blister rising on my thumb. I was surprised at how effective it was, the instant relief from the sadness that had filled the house for so long.

Of course I realized the absurdity of it, a forty-six-year-old man with his blanket. I pulled my thumb out of my mouth and piled the objects back in the box, laying the blanket on top. But try as I might I couldn't get the flaps to close. I left the box open and slid it under the wardrobe rack with my foot. The attic fan pushed a breeze into the sweltering room. I opened my shirt and let the air dry the sweat on my chest and under my arms.

As I turned to head downstairs, I felt something catch me around the ankle and pull. It was a worn strand of yarn that had unraveled from the blanket. I kicked off my loafer and rolled the yarn off my foot. My shirt was drenched. I took it off and dried my back. And as I turned again to leave, I felt a tightening around my other ankle. Another piece of yarn had attached itself. I looked over at the box. The blanket was creeping up over the top, rolling toward me, slapping against my feet and rising up my legs. I lay on the floor and felt the blood rushing to my head. It wrapped itself across my chest and waist. My eyes glazed and I was taken someplace, to a crevice of a memory. I lay there, covered, for hours, until I said, No more, and left the attic, locking all the doors.

Later, when I woke after a feverish dream, I saw that the blanket had found its way into the bed next to me. I yielded. I had to. I rubbed my face in its softness, breathed in the smell, and tangled my fingers in the loose weave, on and on.

So it continued. When I woke in a sweat, there it was, wrapped around me. No matter where I put it, hid it, stuffed it, it always found me. It came creeping back in the dark; out of the blackness I could see it crawling toward me, inching up, rising on the bed, unfolding on my chest, and I would say no to all of it: to the blanket, to my fingers caressing the material, to my thumb that went in my mouth. I'd strip it off my pajamas, the room so dry in the morning heat that the air would fill with a shower of crackling static electrical sparks. I'd shove it in a drawer, exhausted, panting, disgusted with myself, swearing that next time I'd be able to resist.

I hadn't been told I was losing my job, but the firm yanked my hockey tickets—the tickets my father had had, and my grandfather before him, since 1946. They gave my tickets to Wyman. "Wyman needs them for business," they said. "He's on a roll. Brings in business like shit draws flies." And now they were going to find out I was losing Torvin & Mays, the biggest account I'd inherited. I'd lost a substantial portion of my father's book already. I never had his magnetism.

I took Carl Sotterling, Torvin's CFO, to lunch at Mandy's, the place Dad took clients. He winked when he shook my hand. He told me the affection he had for my father—indeed, he said my grandfather had given him his first job. He asked about the health of my mother. He seemed genuinely concerned. I thought I could get him to stay. I was wrong. "We're not getting good execution. You're missing market trends. I'm not asking for a crystal ball, son, but you haven't put us in a hedge, swap, cap, or dollar roll that's worked for over a year."

I would have to go to a less aggressive shop, where the hall carpets weren't whisked away at the slightest sign of wear, to a shop perhaps not disreputable but one that fought for business the major firms deemed not quite first tier. My friends, my father, my grandfather had all been big bulge. I would have to go to a bucket shop.

Back in the office, my briefcase stayed closed on my desk. I didn't take calls. I sat all afternoon waiting for the hand of Max Butterfield, my managing director, to come down on my shoulder. He'd say, "Steve, we need to talk." It was four o'clock. The phones were quiet. The secretaries were in the conference room throwing a baby shower.

After a while, I closed my door, opened my briefcase, and looked in at the blanket. I smoothed my hand over the top and bent my neck to smell it. I lifted it out and spread it, held it to the light. The holes were bigger than the actual material, which had unraveled in places or simply rotted away. It felt small. And then without thinking I started touching and rubbing, and my office and all the offices around me dissolved.

A buzz on the intercom snapped my neck forward. It was

the hospital, calling about whether they should continue my mother's treatment.

Dr. Naylor met me in her room. We looked at her. Her eyes were closed, her chest filling and falling slowly without rhythm. The doctor handed me a clipboard and I signed the DNR order.

"I've put her on ten milligrams." He pointed to the square button on her morphine pump. "I've written an order for thirty." I nodded. "I'm going out for coffee."

"What?" I asked. "You're leaving me here? Alone?"

"You can adjust the dose."

"We all thought she'd go on forever." Mrs. Reingold, a neighbor, handed me a paper plate of ham and Swiss squares on the ends of frilly toothpicks.

I left the plate on the rolltop desk in the library and moved into the living room. My father's partners, my bosses now, were in a huddle by the art books, each with his own plate of square food, all talking at once with full mouths. Max Butterfield, the managing director, stood rigid among them, not talking, not eating, nodding at me across the room when we made eye contact. By now he was certain to have found out about Torvin & Mays. Sotterling sat next to him at the funeral. They were going to let me grieve, give me the week, then give me the ax. Fine. Let it happen.

The women from my mother's investment club sat on the overstuffed chairs and couches; my mother's cleaning lady cried alone on the stairs. Greg Wyman, the proud owner of my hockey tickets, was edging into the circle of partners, sidling up to Butterfield. Carl Sotterling dipped ham square after ham square into a ceramic dish of honey mustard.

Over by the fireplace I saw the Butterfield sisters. I broke into a sweat. They were back to back, talking to other neighbors. I hadn't seen them in years. Victoria was still the plainer of the sisters but was now vaguely attractive, something I had recently become more comfortable with than her sister Robin's brand of overtly sexual beauty.

Robin stepped into the path of her two boys, who were racing through the rooms, sweating through Brooks for Boys oxford cloth, and reminded them that this was a somber occasion. Then she noticed me. "Steve." Bangle bracelets jingling as she rushed over, she held me tight around the neck. "She was a second mom to me." I smelled Diorissimo, honeysuckle. "And this house"—she looked around—"a second home."

"Oh, yes, your mom was the one we went to during my parents' divorce." Victoria had stepped up to my left and I was between them, my tongue balled in my mouth. I was able to hide my unease by appearing to be overcome with grief while the sisters chatted on about Mom and the house, oblivious to the memory of which I was so distinctly aware: a twelve-year-old Robin staring up at the ceiling of the Butterfields' rec room, her mouth making circles around a wad of banana taffy, while I lay between her thighs, illuminating her vagina with a Boy Scout flashlight, dreaming of the darkness within. Victoria had been an equally willing model. Would do it for free. But for Robin it was business: candy for a display. And it was Robin I wanted to look at.

"So how's life at Silverman?" Victoria asked. I put my hand in my pants pocket and fingered the key to the steamer trunk where I'd locked the blanket.

"I'm thinking of looking around. Testing the waters for a smaller shop."

"What? Leave the big bulge?" Victoria asked.

"No!" Robin said.

"Silverman without an Armistead?"

"Dad'll be so disappointed."

I shrugged. "Big bulge doesn't mean that much anymore. Anyway, I've gotten some offers that may be too good to turn down." The two women shook their heads, insisting I was way too valuable, saying, "You mustn't even consider it" and "Put it out of your mind this instant," as though I'd never been between their legs, as though my hips had never rubbed against their mother's gray exercise mat.

A crash in the library sent Robin off to stop the boys. They were accosting each other with fire irons. I was left with Victoria, in need of something to break the silence. I gestured toward the food table.

"No one's eating the duck."

"It's a little hard to cut. You know. Lap food." I appreciated her honesty.

"This is the type of thing my mother handled so well. She'd have known what to serve."

"You've done a fine job."

"No one will ever love me that much again." I don't know where that came from, I just blurted it out. Victoria touched my arm. I started to cry. She reached up and put her arms around my shoulders. I cried and shook in a way I hadn't since I was a small boy, crying into my mother's lap. But now I was bent over, nearly doubled, crying into Victoria. People gathered around me, put their hands on me, told me it was okay to cry, to get it all out. I looked up from Victoria's head and saw her father talking to Sotterling and they were looking at me. I straightened up and wiped my eyes on a napkin. Butterfield put his fingers in the pockets of his jacket and walked over.

"Steve. I know it's not the best time."

The son-of-a-bitch, he was actually going to can me right there at my mother's funeral. Victoria withdrew into the crowd in the kitchen. Butterfield came in close to my ear.

"You're my new director of asset-backed securities. I want you on the ninth floor near me." He pulled a handkerchief out of his pocket and dried his eyes. Then he looked at the coat of arms over the dining room fireplace. "I always want an Armistead near me."

Victoria and I moved through the rooms carrying black trash bags, collecting cups and plates. In the space between the kitchen and dining room we came together and kissed. I led her upstairs to my parents' room. She pulled the belt of her wrap-around dress, let it open and drop on the floor. Then she lay on my grandmother's satin quilt and held her arms up to me. I got on top of her and kissed her again, softly, deeply, then ferociously. I couldn't stop. I couldn't get enough. I dug my tongue deep into her mouth. She made a choking sound and pushed up on my chest.

"I'm sorry," I said. I too was out of breath. "I haven't been with anyone in a long time."

"No. It's okay. Just wanted to look at you." She combed my hair behind my ears. "I've always had a thing for you."

"Oh?"

She nodded. "You always wanted Robin."

"No, no. I liked *you*." She knew I was lying.

"Remember what we used to do?" I felt ashamed and embarrassed. I wished she hadn't mentioned it. "I still think about it."

I started moving on top of her. She opened her legs. I closed my eyes, and the image of Robin licking taffy off her lips, her legs wide apart, came to me as it had hundreds of thousands of times before. I stood and unbuttoned my pants. Victoria kicked her ivory string-bikini underwear off her ankle. I got back on top of her and started kissing her neck, rubbing against her, smelling her perfume.

"Mmm. What are you wearing?"

"Sahara." But it wasn't Sahara I was smelling. It was honeysuckle and Shalimar, catalpa, urine, and sweat. The blanket was on the bed, under Victoria's waist. I jolted back, but a strand of yarn caught me at the base of my penis.

"No!" she snapped. "I don't like that." The head of my penis was ramming against her anus. I tried to stop but I was being yanked. "I said stop!" I was banging against her and calling out in pain. The more I tried to push away from her, the harder I got pulled. She pushed up on me and scratched me in the face. "You son-of-a-bitch!"

She swung out of the bed and gathered her clothes. The yarn from the blanket was still tight around my penis. I lay back and watched it pull tighter. I was in so much pain I couldn't speak. I tried to roll the yarn off, but where one string left off another began. It was all one big tangle around my crotch and midsection; I was trying to fight my way out of a cobweb. With the blanket still attached to me, I chased Victoria out of the room.

"I'm sorry," I called after her on the stairs. "I've never done that with anybody. It's not my thing."

She glanced back at me. I must have looked ridiculous, as if I were wearing a kilt or a loincloth. In the vestibule, she rewrapped her dress and held up her hand for me not to come near her. Then she stumbled out the door.

I raced into the kitchen in search of something sharp to cut off the yarn. One by one, I nicked at the threads around my penis with a paring knife until finally I'd clipped enough so I could rip the rest of the strand with my fingers. The blanket dropped. I fell back against the counter, moaning in relief. Then I looked down at the blanket, which was bunched up into a little tepee on the floor. I grabbed it in my fist and started slashing it with the knife, trying to slice through it, as though I were disemboweling an animal. After I'd spiked it with the knife, right through the linoleum, I ran upstairs for my clothes and went after Victoria.

Racing around corners in my mother's New Yorker, challenging other cars to drive faster, I was crazy to find her. I felt I had to get to her, that I couldn't go another minute without her. It was more than forgiveness; I had to have her. At the intersection of Burnbranche and Spruce, I smelled my mother. And her mother. And all the other smells. I slammed down on the brake with my foot, whipped around, and clenched the blanket in my fist. "What the hell are you doing in my car? What the hell do you want from me?" I shook it as though I were trying to throttle its neck. I tried to stretch it apart with my hands. I smacked it against the window, then shoved it under the seat and stamped on the accelerator. In the middle of the intersection, I made a U-turn and headed for the lake.

I left the car in the parking lot of the waterfront restaurant and shot down to the beach. On the sand, I spread the blanket and weighted down the edges. I found some stones, a half-empty bottle of oil, a waterlogged tennis ball, a soggy sneaker, and a can of paint thinner. I put everything into the center of the blanket and tied off the ends with the lace from the sneaker. Then I lifted the bundle, swung it over my head, and let go. It flew out over the water and sank into the lake.

The water calmed. A boat honked on the horizon. I looked around. It was a perfect spot. The moon shone on the lake, the wedge of light spreading the dark like a woman standing with her legs apart. Behind me there were couples having dinner and drinking at the restaurant. A woman had her foot up on the guardrail; her date was making her laugh. I decided to bring Victoria here. I'd make her laugh too.

Then I noticed a bad smell around me. First, like wet wool, then a rotting marshy smell, then human feces. It was everywhere: in the grasses and shrubs, in the air. I smelled my shirt. It was on me too. I felt what I thought was sweat running down my neck, but it was also moving up. Sand lice. I swiped at my neck and slapped my chest, whipped off my shirt and batted myself down. I hurried over to the car at the edge of the lot.

Driving to Victoria's the smell became more pronounced,

like blood or a dead animal. I felt something crawling in my nose; I tried blowing it into a tissue. Then I sensed something in my ear. Everything itched. Everything burned. I swung the car 180 degrees and headed back to the lake.

From the restaurant, people were leaving in twos, going home to have sex, to wake up together and read the *Times.* I trudged through the waist-deep water, sinking in the muck up to my calves. The sludge sucked the shoes right off my feet when I pulled up my legs. There was oil floating on the surface, a piece of wood with a protruding nail, rotting fruit peels, a condom. I made a deal that if I found the blanket I would donate five hours a week to cleaning up this mess, to making our waters and coasts more beautiful. I would leave my job, give my life to cleaning up the filth. I arrived at what I believed was the point of entry and went under. I waved my arms through the gunk and came up gasping and fighting my need to puke. Again, I filled my lungs with air and surface-dived to the bottom. I grabbed whatever grass root or rock or car part that could move me along the bottom, my arms stretching, my hands searching, smoothing over the mud. I came up choking and empty-handed.

Collapsed on the beach, I wanted to sink into the mud and sand forever. My eyes burned and teared. I was drenched and cold but too crippled to move. Water lapped at my feet. The sand buried my ankles.

Then I felt it. I looked down. The blanket was across my legs. I fingered the wet, frayed material. I embraced it. It felt small and spent. I held on to what was left. I touched and rubbed and sucked. The world blurred. We lay on the dirty beach for a long time. Stillness on the water came and went with passing boats. The restaurant closed. I heard women's voices, ignitions turning over, motors fading away. A couple who had been making love in the grass nearby climbed out and stepped right over me. Sometime during the night, the clouds covered the moon. We stretched out side by side, together in the dark, hidden.

Beauty and Rudy

"Rudy flew a Piper Arrow with a ton of the finest Mexican money can buy and crashed and burned in the Everglades," Gil said, driving out of the woods and back onto I-95 in a maraschino Impala. "They say the heat from the fire melted a medallion with the sun, the moon, and the planets on it, and now he's got the solar system branded on his chest." Gil looked at Stan in the rearview. "They say there're some pretty free women up there, Stanley. And some folks into astroprojection—you know, out-of-body type stuff. Something I mean to try."

"*Astral* projection isn't real," Beauty said, trying to rub the pounding of a nitrous hangover from her temples.

"People think it's a crock because nothing ever materializes," Gil said. "But things *have* materialized."

"Like what?" Beauty wished she could get in the back seat with Stan.

"Oh, semiprecious stones, keepsakes. They say out at Rudy's farm a strand of pearls materialized on a chair."

"Are there going to be any drugs there?" Beauty cradled the bright blue nitrous tank in her lap. " 'Cause I got to get off the N, Gil. The N's making me dotty. My brain's ba-booming around in my bean like a cat in the dryer."

"Have I ever seared you wrong, Beauty?"

"Steered, idiot. S-T-E-E-R-E-D."

What a tiny delicate jewel she was: five feet tall and everybody wanted to touch her. Her mother thought she should be on TV and arranged a job doing the ads for Big Bob's Bad Boy Toyota and Used. Beauty the Big Bob Girl was how she was known around Hollywood, Florida. Big Bob said he'd do anything to sell you a car. But it was Beauty who shot out of the cannon, kissed the monkey, and flew on top of the airplane. Beauty told Big Bob that if he ever exposed himself to her again she'd go to the Consumer Protection Agency about the rolled-back mileage on some of those used cars. But Big Bob couldn't resist apple cheeks, apple breasts, an apple bottom. And so, after ransacking the back office, Beauty accepted Gil's invitation north, where he promised to siphon off her blues.

"This is it?" Beauty rifled through the box of groceries Stan and Gil brought out from the Buck 'n' Dough. "This is all you got?"

"That and this." Gil showed her the contents of the Buck 'n' Dough cash register.

"I can't eat any of this."

"There's lots of good stuff. Snowballs, Ho Ho's, Vienna sausage, soup." Gil opened a can of Chicken & Stars.

"How're we supposed to heat it up?"

Gil bent back his neck and poured the can of Chicken & Stars in his mouth. First in was the broth, flecked with solidified chicken fat; then came the stars, which slipped out of the can in one gelatinous disk and blopped in his mouth, splattering soup all over the windshield.

"I hate you. I wish you were dead." Beauty kicked her foot through the glove compartment.

Gil unwound the hose of the nitrous tank, forced Beauty's head down, pried open her jaw, plunged the end of the hose in her mouth, and made her suck tank until she slumped down in the seat, happy.

"There's no pleasing that woman, Stanley," Gil said, opening a can of Bean with Bacon, "no matter how I try. I tell her about the pyramids, semiotics. All she wants to do is bang. Consider yourself lucky."

Stan lit a new Old Gold from an old one and finished picking out the coupons from the Old Gold cartons they took from the Buck 'n' Dough. He was only seven thousand coupons away from the Winnebago. Gil had no idea just how lucky Stan was.

Proceeding without knowing the direction, the travelers chanced upon the ferry that took them across the choppy sound and around the curvy roads of Firefly Island. Arriving at Rudy's farm, Beauty saw rows and rows of fruit trees and life-size statues the color of human flesh with green-painted genitals. On closer examination, Beauty saw that they weren't statues at all but guests of the farm, involved in various forms of free love and tai chi. One couple was in a position that Beauty used to laugh at before she met Gil.

When Beauty, Gil, and Stan stepped out of the Impala, some mischievous goats tried to butt them back in. Beauty screamed and held on tightly to the nitrous tank; the goats *bah-h-hhed* with delight. But then the sky darkened and the goats ran away. Across the farm a man came walking, a man so frightful to look at the travelers were ready to faint with fear. *Was* it a man? It had the shape of a man but the skin of a beast. Tufts of hair grew here and there on its back, front, and head through thick grafts of skin and scar tissue. Beauty could see that half its face was extraordinarily handsome. But the other half was buried in a zigzag of scars. Its chest was as scarred as its face, and its back was as scarred as its front. Beauty knew if she blew chunks now, she'd blow and she'd blow and she'd blow herself inside out.

Rudy walked right up to her. They always know, Beauty thought.

"Scared?" the beast said in its terrible voice.

"No." She started to feel her saliva thin, preparing her mouth for regurgitated Burger King.

"Touch it," Rudy said.

Trying to hide her fear, Beauty touched its chest with her finger.

"Youch!" Rudy recoiled like her finger was a red-hot shish kebab skewer. Then he laughed and slapped five with the men, and the goats came out from behind the trees to butt the guests, and the sky brightened. Beauty kecked Whopper on Gil's shoes.

"Don't let that scaly old beast bother you," Linda, a nice woman in lots of Hindu print clothing, said. "He's got a good heart." Linda held Beauty's head in her lap and stroked her hair and gave her parsley tea for the nausea.

"Stan and I are gettin' off the N," Beauty said, happy to have some female companionship. "Really. I'm gonna suck this tank and then we're definitely gettin' off."

"Shh," Linda said.

All around her, people spoke of nothing but Rudy. Beauty heard snippets as she fell in and out of consciousness.

". . . a firebomb in Greenwich Village. Rudy was trapped in the basement for two days."

". . . lit himself on fire to protest the war."

". . . used to wear an Indian peace symbol . . ."

". . . Nepalese temple balls around his neck . . ."

". . . the search party who found him said they . . ."

". . . glowed red like liquid steel."

Beauty dreamed she was a player token in the game of Mystery Date, moving door-to-door looking for the Guy in the Dinner Jacket. But behind every door was the Dud. But then she realized the Dud was the most handsome of all the dates. Surely the Dud was Stan, Beauty thought.

Beauty skipped through the orchard because Stan loved her. She picked an apple but it was wormy so she dropped it.

"The Koran said it was a banana," Rudy said.

Beauty was startled by his unexpected appearance in a tree.

"What?" she asked.

Rudy disappeared from the tree and appeared standing in front of her. "The forbidden fruit. The Koran said it was a banana." She tried not to look at his scars but couldn't help it. "I lit myself on fire," he said. Beauty thought she'd faint. Rudy laughed that she believed him. "I was a lucky Pinto owner," he explained. "I bought this farm with the settlement money. Are you all right?" He touched her arm. She slid away. "Why do you shudder when I come near you?"

"I don't," she said.

"I like physical closeness." He moved closer. She could feel his horrible breath on her face and her saliva thinning again in her mouth.

"How come you're not astral projecting with the others?" she asked, and stepped sideways.

"Because I think it's a crock," Rudy said.

"They say a strand of pearls materialized on a chair."

"I put them there."

"I have to get back."

"To Gil?" Rudy asked. "Or is it Stan?" Beauty was speechless. "Don't be misled by appearances, Beauty."

"You don't know them," she said.

"I know you," he whispered.

"They say you had sex with a dog."

"I loved her," Rudy said, and disappeared before her eyes.

"Hook 'im, cook 'im," Gil said. "The Cinder. I'm tired of moving around. I want the farm."

"I'm not hookin' the Cinder," Beauty said.

"Why not?" Gil said.

"Because it'll make me sick. And I'm not gonna cook."

"Fine," Gil said. "You hook, Stan'll cook."

"Why do I gotta hook at all? Why can't you just cook without the hook?"

" 'Cause he's sneaky, the Cinder. Got eyes all over his body. And he likes you."

Beauty hoped Gil would die soon.

Beauty was startled by the sudden appearance of Rudy by the pond. "What are you doing?" she asked.

"Going for a swim," he said, naked. Beauty looked around for Stan, to see if he was waiting in the woods for the cook. "Coming?" Rudy asked. Beauty pretended to be shy about taking off her clothes. "Dang," Rudy said. "You debs from the South."

"I'm not from the South," Beauty said. "I'm from Florida." Peeking, Beauty noticed the part of Rudy that had been spared the Pinto explosion. "And besides, it's freezing. Aren't you freezing?"

"Scar tissue doesn't get cold. Feel it." He took her hand. She pulled away. He laughed.

"You're always trying to scare me," Beauty said. "But I'm not afraid of you, Rudy. I walk under an umbrella of protection, the love of the man I love: Stan. You shouldn't laugh at people, and you shouldn't try to scare people. It isn't nice." Beauty surprised herself as much as Rudy.

And then Rudy didn't look scary anymore. He started to cry, big acid tears that burned through the earth and dripped out over the Seychelle Islands and landed on the bald spot of the British explorer Sir Peregine Pomsomby-Smythe's head. "Bleedin' birds," Peregine said.

"I know I do things that scare people," Rudy cried. "And I act superior, but I can't help it. The physical pain left over from the accident makes me irritable, and people expect to be afraid of me so I give them what they want. If I don't, they'll stop coming and then I'll have no one."

Rudy cried and cried, and more tears burned through the earth.

"You know," Rudy said, wiping his eyes with an asbestos mitt, "I used to be a pretty good-looking guy."

"You're still—"

"Don't give me false compliments, Beauty. I hate them. I'm deformed and hideous."

"You're not so bad," Beauty said. "Why, with the right hairstyle . . ." She wet her fingers and tried to smooth down his hair, but no matter how much saliva she greased on his head, the hairs popped back up like inflatable-clown toys.

"Could you ever love me?" he asked.

"No."

"Is my company so contemptible?"

"Oh, no."

"Try?" He unzipped her cutoffs.

"I-I-I," she said, "I'm not into this."

"Get into it," he said. "Get into me." He pulled off her cutoffs and knelt at her feet.

It's a shame, she thought, that he is so ugly, for he is so good.

"I don't see why you had to kill him," Beauty said.

Stan had run a chef's knife through Gil's ear. The first knife had done little, and he'd had to run another through Gil's other ear. Gil was in the process of an out-of-body experience when he saw two chef's knives sticking out of his head. "Guess I ain't coming back," Gil said.

Everything was better with Stan. Gil had stuck it in, shot off, and didn't go south. Stan could dry-hump for hours and ate Beauty like filet. Gil yacked and yacked: "I invented the bacon cheeseburger, you know. At Smiley's on Route Four. I said, Smiley, throw some bacon on that burger, and so it was." Gil thought he was funny: "I believe in parallel universes, and in one of them are your missing car keys." Stan was a mute. But now that Gil was gone, everything seemed different. Too tired to raise her pelvis to meet Stan's anymore after a three-hour dry hump, Beauty went to sleep and had a nitrous dream that she was a Chinese man rowing a boat through the bloodstream of a Chinese man rowing a boat through the bloodstream of a Chinese man rowing a boat through the bloodstream of a Chinese man rowing a boat.

"Here's what you're looking at, Toots," Detective Mallory said. "You got your two consecutive life sentences for the murders of Robert Buck Brown aka Big Bob and the unidentifiable owner of a '64-model maraschino Impala, and you got your big three-0 for conspiracy. *Capisce?*"

"I'm telling you I don't know where Stan is," Beauty cried.

"Look, Honey Pot." Mallory's voice became gentle. "I got a gift set of six ginsus with two unaccounted for. If you're trying to harbor this Stan character, keep it in your toboggan [he meant noggin] he doesn't give a rat's hooey for you."

Beauty's mouth formed an upside-down crescent moon, and she cried so hard no sound came out.

Mallory rubbed his face. Time was when he knew every license plate on the rock. Trouble? He could seal the place—stop the ferries, the barges, nobody comes or goes—with a phone call. But since these Rudy people came, the rock was an open sore, wide open for any two-bit pathogenic opportunistic infection to pus up. It was the Rudy people who burned his house while he was off playing a clown for the brats at the policemen's benevolence picnic. All he owned now was what he had on his back. The big ruffled collar made his neck itch.

"Somebody's got to answer for Gil," he whispered, and lit an exploding cigar.

Beauty looked up at the ceiling of the barn. There must have been a hundred thousand fireflies up there, oxidizing and glowing, oxidizing and glowing. Luciferin. Heatless light. They use it to attract one another. Rudy taught her that. She remembered how she used to collect them in a jar when she was a little girl and let them go in her room. They'd be dead in the morning.

"No," Rudy said, entering her. "Just sleeping; they're nocturnal." Beauty hated it when he read her mind without asking. She hated the sweat between his scales, the way he'd be nice to animals and then eat them, that he had to have sex every seven minutes. She was starting to miss Stan again. Even Gil, a little bit.

"Hold your horses, I'll get them," Rudy said, climbing the ladder to the loft of the barn.

"Get what?"

"You were about to say, You stupid idiot, get me my Seconals."

"I was not."

"You were too."

Beauty wished he'd shut up and die.

"*You* shut up," Rudy said.

"You shut up, you stupid idiot, and get me my Seconals."

Rudy stood at the top of the loft with a fresh erection and threw down the bottle of Seconals. Beauty held up her hand and squeezed it shut, hoping the bottle would end up there, but it landed in the hay and opened and the little pills rolled into the abyss. Beauty started to cry.

"I wish you were dead," she cried, over and over, pounding the hay with her fists.

Rudy took her in his arms and kissed her face.

"There, there, don't cry, Beauty. Isn't this better than jail? You saw that Linda Blair movie. Say, how 'bout I go to the dentist for a fresh tank? Would that make it better?"

Beauty nodded, put her arms around him, and kissed the Jupiter brand on his chest for luck. She felt better.

"Now," Rudy said. "How 'bout that blow job?"

"Get out! Get out! Get out!" Beauty screamed.

Dang, that woman gets mad faster than any woman I've

ever seen, Rudy thought, as he walked into the warm sunshine looking for his favorite goat. Must be the macrobiotic
diet she put herself on. "Seen Timmy?" he asked a steer. The
steer tilted his head in the direction of the sugar house. Come
to think of it, the whole last millennium together had been a
bitch.

Rare Is a Cold Red Center

There's a girl who comes in the restaurant Thursdays and Fridays, and if I'm lucky the hostess will put her where I can look at her face. She comes to the salad bar, which is a horseshoe around the grill, gets her lettuce, some chick peas, purple onion, and dressing. Creamy vinaigrette. She's slow through the line and people get impatient. But that's one thing I like about her. She's careful with the food.

She wears short-sleeve sweaters, which I don't understand. You wear a sweater to keep warm but then your arms are left out in the cold. Sometimes she wears a yellow one, which is fuzzy and pieces of it come off in the air.

I work the grill with Mohammed but he goes by his American name, which is Alfred. Alfred wears a turban. He doesn't have to wear a chef's hat on the grounds of religion. I try to talk to Alfred to pass the time.

"Alfred, gonna watch the game tonight?" I say.

"No," he says.

"Not a sports fan?"

"Ninety percent of the players are black. I lose interest."

I wish they'd put Jim on the grill so I'd have somebody to talk to.

Jim and I share a room at Sunrise, the halfway house. They won't let Jim up front because of his skin. He's been through a couple of windshields and he's got pretty bad acne. Something's always bleeding on his face. They don't want customers to see him touching the food, so he works in the back, cutting up lettuce for the salad bar, filling up dressing tubs, bringing out burger patties. No one talks to Jim. If somebody needs to say something to Jim, they tell me and I tell Jim. Howard Lippman the manager, How-Weird the Lip Man, said, "Corky, why don't you tell Jim to do something about his skin? There's stuff you can do for that." Jim just doesn't care about his skin. Not a priority.

"Corky?" It's Mary, one of the waitresses. "I need a favor." I owe a debt to Mary. I took her home after work once, made love to her, and then didn't want it to go any further. "Will you take an order down to Mac?"

None of the girls want to go down to Mac because of the things he says to them. Mac's the black guy who works the ovens in the basement. If somebody orders the flounder or an omelet it goes down to Mac. It's hot down there, and there's no ventilation. Once I said, "Mac, how do you stand it?"

"You know how," Mac says.

"No, I don't," I say.

Mac whispers, " 'Cause a nigger can get used to anything."

I pretend I don't hear and pick up the food.

"You heard me," he says.

Rare is a cold red center. Medium-rare is a hot red center. Medium is a pink center. And medium-well is cooked through. There's no well-done unless someone sends back medium-well, and then we cook the hell out of it. The girl orders well-done. Once I undercooked so she'd send back and I could see where she bit, what condiments she used. She uses ketchup. Afterward, I felt like that was wrong, like I was peeking in on her. It's personal, how people fix and eat their food. But when I touched her burger, I was touching something she touched, something I'd made that she touched with her hands and mouth, and it made me shake a bit. I wonder if she thought about that too.

I give my time card to How-Weird and remind him about his promise to try me out waitering. He's been holding that over my head, making me put that stupid chef's hat back on when the girl comes in, checking my time card to make sure nobody else punched in for me. He also knows I live at Sunrise, which is no great help. How-Weird's got his assistant in his office, Ellen. Ellen always looks like she's been crying. Everybody knows How-Weird's doing her even though he's married. She's always in there saying, "Howard, Howard, leave her." I know because his office is right next to the bar and Tom, our bartender, is always listening and tells everybody what they say and what they do. He says there's nothing they haven't done in that office. Nothing.

In the morning Jim and I form the burgers. There's a barrel of meat and a scale. We put twelve ounces in each patty mold. The meat's so cold your hands get numb. After touching it so much, it doesn't seem like meat anymore, from an animal. Jim's a pretty good artist, and he'll mold some of the meat into the shape of a chicken or a cow. Once he did a whole tray of cows. Everybody came back to see and thought it was pretty funny. Even Mac came up from downstairs. How-Weird docked Jim an hour's wage for the time spent making the cows, and Mary didn't laugh at all because she's a vegetarian.

I remember that day because I walked Mary home after work, and she asked if I wanted to see where she lived. Her apartment's filled with lots of Indian print stuff and big pillows. We were kissing on her big pillow couch and I said, "Mary, I like you a lot. I think you're a great girl, I just can't get into anything right now. You know my situation at Sunrise and all."

"And there's that girl who comes into Sir Arthur's. Don't think I don't see."

I felt a little buzz go through me. Somebody knew about the girl, mentioned her. I never even wanted to know the girl's name because I'd have to hear it from somebody else. It would pass over somebody else's lips before mine.

"It's okay," Mary said. "I'm not looking for any big involvement."

I took Mary at her word and kissed her again. Mary was

pretty, but I looked in her shirt and saw that she had strange breasts and lost my erection. I had to close my eyes and think about a girl I met at a party once. It was at a big house with a lot of rich people, and my friend Ron and I crashed. Everybody was doing Placidyl and Jell-O shots. I was leaning against a washing machine drinking a beer, and a girl came up and put her tongue in my mouth and her hand down my pants. Just like that. I was too wasted to get it up and had to think about the first girl I ever loved. Caroline. With Caroline I had to close my eyes and imagine *her*. I imagined Caroline at the beach with her top off, leaning back on a car looking at me, like a picture I'd seen in a magazine. I think sex is always better with someone you love.

Mary didn't give me any trouble afterward but I could tell she would have liked things to be different, like if she were the one to leave right after and I was the one wanting her to stay.

I wait all week for the girl. Monday and Tuesday, nothing. Wednesday I've got to prepare. Thursday she comes in. I feel clumsy and crazy, looking at her hair, watching her laugh at something her friend said, imagining she's laughing at something I said. Friday I'm getting used to having her around and I play a little game, pretending we live in a big house, and I'm cooking dinner for her, and all these customers are our kids and our friends. Then the weekend. Group, park cleanup, study for high school equivalency. Most people at Sunrise have a debt to pay, for something they stole or burned down or for holding. Since I'm voluntary, I don't have to clean up the park, but I walk along with Jim. One day I decide to tell him about the girl.

"What girl?" Jim says.

"She's kind of cross-eyed. You got to know who I mean."

"Fuzzy yellow sweater."

"That's right," I say.

"Tight pussy, clean box."

It's because of these things he says that nobody wants to talk to Jim. He says that particular thing about every girl. He doesn't even know what it means. I'm sure he's never even been with a girl unless he paid her, and I'm pretty certain I would know about it. Jim stabs his poker into a Twinkie wrapper on the grass. At least I got it off my chest.

In rehab they tell you that you wish somebody would turn you in and you put yourself into situations where you know you'll get caught. I never got caught. One night my friend Ron and I took a car from the Park & Lock on Cordell, a convertible Dodge, and drove to Beltsville, where we heard some people were cooking up base in a farmhouse and we wanted to give it a try. Ron worked for a vet and had a steady supply of dog Valium. We ate nine dog Valiums each and split a six of Ballantine tallboys. I held some meth on the end of a key under Ron's nose and he drove into the back of a van.

I flew out. All I remember is walking through the woods saying my brother's name over and over: Barry. I hadn't even seen him for four years. I came out of the woods and lights were spinning around. I walked around five cop cars to get to Ron. They had him bent over the hood of one of the cars and were treating him pretty rough, picking up his head by his hair and slamming it down on the hood.

I walked over to him, through a circle of six cops, and said, "Ron, man, what do you want me to do with the car?"

Ron said, "I don't know, man." He spit some blood.

Then I asked the cops if they'd seen a set of keys. They looked all around with flashlights, under the cars, in the front seat of the Dodge, said they hadn't seen any keys, and took Ron off.

I had a phone number in my jacket for Helping Hands, a detox clinic. They came and picked me up at a Hardee's on Route 1.

It's Thursday, and I try to stay asleep as long as I can. I don't like having empty time on my hands while I'm waiting for the girl. As always, when I wake up, Jim's awake, lying in bed smoking. I remind him the meat comes in today and we've got to unload it and separate it into bins. I put on jeans, a flannel shirt, and the army jacket I got from my brother Barry. Jim's been wearing the same black jeans for a week and a half now, a designer brand with yellow stitching somebody donated to Sunrise.

"A little ripe," I say.

"Yeah," Jim says.

It's cold and windy, and Jim and I walk with our hands in our pockets and our heads down. Jim lights a Marlboro and shakes one from the pack for me. I hope it's not too busy today so I can look at the girl in peace.

The meat delivery's late so Jim forms the patties while Mac

and I unload. Mac is pissed off at having to unload, so he tries to irritate me by singing the same lyrics over and over—"Got the Funk. Got the Funk. Got the F-F-U-N-K. Got the Funk. Got the Funk. Got the F-F-U-N-K"—looking at me the whole time, waiting for me to get irritated. But after a while I've heard it so many times I don't notice anymore.

I check on Jim. He's worked fast, and he's got eight trays done already. But I look at the patties, and he's shaped them all like hearts. One hundred and sixty twelve-ounce hearts.

"For Valentine's Day, man."

"Oh, Jim, man." I think it's a nice idea, something the customers will really enjoy. Then I remember we work for How-Weird. "Sorry, man," I say.

We've got to start the whole thing over, press the hearts in the molds. Jim doesn't mind that we have to wreck his work. He's whistling and singing and working faster than I've ever seen. He's weighing and slapping the meat in the molds and I can't keep up—if anything, I'm slowing him down—so I step back, have a smoke, let him do the work, and he doesn't even mind.

"What's with you, Jim?" I say.

Jim wipes his hands on his pants, opens up his pocket, and shows me a prescription bottle of little yellow pills. It's got How-Weird's name on it.

"Bullshit," I say.

"No shit," Jim says. "Everybody ate some."

"If they find out at Sunrise you're shit-canned," I say.

"It's Valentine's Day," Jim says.

I go out in the restaurant, and everybody seems cheerful and friendly while they're setting up the tables. Mary's not laying any trips on me, and all the girls seem happy in their work like it's the first day of spring. Even Alfred is at the grill singing that old song by K.C. and the Sunshine Band, "Get Down Tonight." I can't believe it.

"Did you have some of Jim's Valentine candy?" Alfred asks.

"No, I didn't have any of Jim's Valentine candy," I say, but Alfred's already leaning over the salad bar, chitchatting with Mary like old friends.

Jim's filling up the salad bar and looking at me, waiting for me to say I want some of the Desoxyn. I just pay attention to what I'm doing. Get the grill hot. Set up my order board. I came up with the idea for the order board. The girls stick the orders on the nail, and I put them on the board in the exact position where the burger or steak will go on the grill. Just pay attention. One minute at a time. Shit. I'm never going to get through today with all these people speeding. "Jim," I say. . . .

At eleven-fifteen the older customers come in. I know what they want, so I can put their burgers on before they order. The place is filling up. Everybody wants to go out to lunch for Valentine's Day. I look at Alfred and see his forehead sweating. Coldest day of the year so far, and Alfred's sweating like it's July. I'm about to rib him for it when I hear my heart. My heart's pounding so hard I think everybody can hear it. I can't breathe. I've got to slow it down.

I run over to the bar for a shot of something. Tom's busy. Everybody wants a whiskey sour. Tom tells Mary to tell the customers the blender's broken so he won't have to make piña coladas. I've got to rush back to the grill and tell Alfred to watch my burgers.

"Alfred, one to seven rare. Eight and nine medium-rare. Ten to twelve well."

"Eight and nine medium?" he asks. I started to cook before the orders came in so there's nothing on the board. I've got to go through the orders on the nail: MR, MR, MW, MR, R, R, MR, R, R, R, MW. . . .

"There's no medium," I say. "Nothing's medium." I run back over to Tom. "Tom," I say. "Give me something. I'll pay you tomorrow." I've got my hand over my heart because I think it's going to pop out of my shirt.

"It's okay, buddy," Tom says. "You just got butterflies." He pours me a shot from the rail. Tom's a smooth dresser, wears suits with no back vent and a lot of jewelry. He puts Score in his hair and slicks it straight back. He talks about this lady and that lady, and they always want him to take their picture. He's got pictures of this chick with the biggest breasts I've ever seen. Everybody knows he paid her.

The shot is hot going down. I never liked the taste of booze. I have to fight the urge to puke. My heart slows a bit and I feel hot all over.

"You're okay." He pats my wrist. "It's just butterflies." Tom had some of the Desoxyn too.

I go back to the grill and I'm starting to feel okay. I get a feeling from long ago, a sense of overall well-being. The rare is out and I'm getting ready to take off the medium-rare. I'm really enjoying my work and seeing the customers happy with their meals.

"Corky." It's Mary. "Tell Jim the lettuce is low and we never got kidney beans or crackers."

I push open the door to the back. Jim's not there. Claudio's doing dishes. "Claudio. *¿Dónde está Jim?*"

"I don't know," Claudio says.

"Tell him we need more lettuce." Nobody eats kidney beans.

It's noon. People have to wait in line for a table.

"Young man," an old man says, "is there more lettuce?"

I take the lettuce bowl in the back. "Claudio . . ."

"Ain't seen him, man."

I go in the walk-in. It feels great because the grill's so hot. I take out five heads of iceberg and break them up in the bowl. "This how Jim does it?" I ask Claudio.

Claudio looks at me, like, How the hell should I know, I just do the dishes.

People are lined up, nearly to the door, when I get back with the lettuce.

"Alfred, my orders," I say. He didn't flip my rare. I'm going to have to move them down to medium and start new ones.

"I've got my own to worry about," Alfred says. He's getting agitated from the Desoxyn.

"Corky." It's Ellen. She looks like she's been crying pretty bad today. "Howard wants to see you."

"Tell him I'll be there soon as I can."

The grill's filled to capacity and there's a wait for new orders. Mary points to the lettuce bowl, which is getting low again, and I just hold up my hands. The lettuce bowl gets

down to almost nothing and I've got to take it in the back. I
see the girl waiting in line with her friend. The shot's worn off
and my heart's starting to pound again. In the walk-in I hold
on to my chest. Just relax. Tom keeps a bottle of Finlandia in
here, and I throw back a swig. Don't puke. Five heads of iceberg. I stay in the walk-in while I break them up. I've got to
rush back to the grill and tell Alfred to watch my burgers.

"Alfred, one to five rare. . . ."

"I got it, I got it."

I go back in the walk-in, finish the iceberg, do another shot
of Finlandia, bring out the lettuce, flip my mediums.

Mary comes over to the grill. "Corky."

I know she wants me to go down to Mac.

"Mary, I got a full grill and Jim's nowhere to be found."

"Please, Corky." She's almost crying. "I just can't deal with
Mac today."

I can't deal with Mac today either, so when I clip the order
to Mac's spin-around I just say "Ordering" and head for the
stairs.

"Just what is this supposed to be?" Mac says, looking at
the order. I knew I wasn't getting away that easy.

"It's an order, Mac, just what it looks like. And if I remember correctly it's an order for stuffed baked flounder."
Mac doesn't say anything. I bolt up the stairs and stop mid-
way. I had no right to talk to Mac that way. "Mac, I'm sorry,"
I say, when I get back down. "It's crazy up there. Everybody's
getting burgers and salad bar and Jim's disappeared."

"Don't matter," Mac says. "It's no different from the way
anybody around here treats me." Mac lays a piece of fish in a
dish and dots it with butter.

"What do you want, Mac?" I say. "How about a Coke? How about I bring you a Coke, my treat?"

Mac shrugs and slips the fish in the oven.

"What do you say, Mac?"

"Yeah," he says. "I'll take the Coke."

When I get back to the grill, Mary and Alfred are arguing. "Corky, I put eleven in ten minutes ago and it hasn't even been put on the grill."

"I never saw it, I never saw it," Alfred says.

"Hang on," I say. I look on the board, I look on the nail. It's still on the nail. "I got it, Mary. I'll put it on now."

Mary runs back to the tables. Alfred says "Cunt" under his breath.

The girl's wearing a light-green sweater.

"Corky." Ellen again.

"Shit, Ellen. I forgot. Alfred . . ."

"Okay, okay, just go," Alfred says. I high-tail it to How-Weird's office.

How-Weird doesn't look up from the papers he's filling out. I just stand there. I take off my chef's hat and hold it like I'm a soldier. Then I think how stupid that is and put it back on. Then I think it's stupid to be standing in an office with a big chef's hat on.

"Was it worth it?" How-Weird asks, still not looking up.

If you're going to shit-can me, shit-can me. "Was what worth it?" I say.

"Dishes, stockroom, working the grill, all your hard work?"

I have nothing to say.

"Mary's leaving," How-Weird says. "You get your shot at waitering."

"Pardon?" I say.

"You heard me. Monday. Three-day trial."

I come out of Howard's office and Tom claps his hands. Ellen gives me a kiss on the cheek. Someone told the old guy at twelve, and he toasts me with his scotch. Lunch has slowed down a bit. I can relax a little, even smoke a cigarette as long as the customers don't see.

There's a hush in the restaurant and then a low buzz of people talking. I think maybe something happened to the grill or Jim walked in the front, but the grill's fine and Jim's still missing. Everybody is looking at an old fat guy with a young chick at seventeen. Tom's away from the bar, walking around with his hands behind his back like he's the manager, looking all over to make sure the place is running smoothly. One of the waitresses mouths something to me. I can't make out what she's trying to tell me, so she comes over to the grill.

"Peter Ustinov," she says.

She points to seventeen. It's the actor Peter Ustinov. He's with a French chick and she wants coffee. He orders a piña colada, and suddenly Tom's blender is working.

I don't know any of the movies Peter Ustinov has been in, so I ask the waitress.

"I don't know any of the names," she says. "A lot of Roman movies."

"Mary," I say, as she's sticking an order on the nail, "What's he been in?"

"I can't remember," she says. Seventeen is Mary's and she's flustered.

The girl is looking over at the actor and talking to her friend. She's snapping her fingers, trying to figure out what movies he's been in.

Tom brings the piña colada out himself. "Here you are, sir. On the house."

I don't know since when Tom can be giving drinks on the house. He comes over to the salad bar and leans on it. His jacket arm slides up over his wrist and a solid gold ID bracelet. He looks around the place like it's his.

"Tom," I say, "what's he been in?" Tom closes his eyes and holds a finger in the air so that no one will disturb him while he's trying to remember. He snaps his fingers a few times. He slaps himself on the forehead.

"You know," Tom says, "he has been featured in so many films. He is our finest living actor, and each of his films has slipped my mind."

"A lot of Roman movies?" I ask.

"Yes, quite a few," Tom says, and then he starts talking about a man of that caliber this and a man of that caliber that and he'll be wanting the New York strip and he'll want it rare.

Mary brings the order. He wants a cheeseburger medium. The French chick wants salad but she doesn't want to go through the line, so Mary puts something together for her.

The girl's looking over here. She moves her lips, trying to say something. I look here and there to see if she's looking at somebody else. Alfred's making the actor's cheeseburger. She's not looking at him. I point to myself. "Me?" I say, no sound coming out.

She mouths something again.

"Me?" I say again. She walks over. I'm seeing spots like I'm about to pass out. She leans over the salad bar.

"A Funny Thing Happened on the Way to the Forum. The actor. He was in that movie." Her eyes are a little crossed, and I'm trying to figure out which one to look in.

"Yeah," I say. "That's it, Alfred, *A Funny Thing Happened on the Way to the Forum.*"

"What?" Alfred couldn't care less.

"Hey, what's your name?" It's not me asking, it's a ghost that looks like me.

"Elizabeth," she says.

"Well . . . ," I can't say the name; it won't go past my lips. "Make yourself at home." I don't know why I said that.

"Thanks," she says, and starts to leave with her friend.

"Hey," I say. She turns around. "Have a good one."

"Thanks," she says. "You too."

I can feel my chest pounding again, but it's not a bad feeling anymore. It's just my heart saying, Yeah, I was happy to see her too.

"Corky." Ellen again. "Howard wants to know where Jim is."

I'm heading out the front when I remember Mac's Coke. He probably doesn't want it anymore. Jim's in the back seat of a maroon Duster. A guy with long wet hair is sitting in the driver's seat wearing a tan jean jacket. I get in the front and Jim introduces Keeko. Keeko calls Jim Jimbo.

"Jim, you're shit-canned at Arthur's. And you know How-Weird's going to tell Sunrise." Jim lights a Marlboro and looks out the window. Keeko starts the car. "Where we going?" I ask. Keeko's heading for the Pike. "We got to get back to Sunrise by five."

"It's four now," Jim says.

"I know," I say. "I just want to make sure we get back by five."

"We're just going downtown, Corky," Jim says.

"This ain't the way downtown," I say. Keeko takes the Beltway ramp toward Frederick. "And we got to get to Sunrise by five."

Keeko makes his voice high and squeaky like a girl and imitates me. "We got to get to Sunrise by five."

Just relax into it. On 270, Keeko's flooring it but so's everybody else, trying to get home, away from wherever they were. I'm feeling kind of hurt. All this time I've known Jim and never knew he went by Jimbo or ever heard about Keeko. Nobody's saying anything. I look at Keeko's face. He looks like he's seen his share of windshields too. I can see how these two are friends. They can hang together all day with their messed-up faces and never say anything. Nobody will want to look at them, and nobody will want to talk to them. Jim puts his hand on my shoulder and squeezes it a little.

On 70 the road narrows and you can see farms with cows and some horses. The sun is low and huge because it's winter and I'm looking at the shadows from the trees. We shoot under the Appalachian Trail Bridge and come to the top of the hill where you first see the mountains over the Middletown valley. It's out here that I'm finally able to say it, let it go past my lips, even if it's just a whisper now: "Elizabeth, Elizabeth."

Pudding

I made it from scratch. I melted the chocolate, beat in the egg, and stirred over low heat with a wooden spoon until it thickened, just how my mother would make it. What a lovely idea, I thought, homemade pudding for my family.

"It's got scum on the top," our son Phin says.

"I'll peel it off for you."

"It tastes a little weird, hon," my husband Dan says quietly.

Phin leaves the table, slouching defiantly over a frame that seems too small to hold up his newly developed man's shoulders.

"Why can't we have a normal dessert?" our daughter Miranda asks. "Like Pepperidge Farm cookies."

I tell her Pepperidge Farm cookies are expensive. And they get eaten too quickly.

"That's what cookies are for," Miranda says. "They're for eating."

"What about you, Anastasia?" I ask. "Do you like the pudding?"

Anastasia is three, with an advanced sense of empathy. She is as concerned with not hurting anyone's feelings as she is with not taking sides, and now I've put her on the spot. She holds her spoon tightly in her fist. Her eyebrows pucker. Her breathing quickens.

"Well? Do you?"

"I don't like pudding," Dan says, as we're cleaning up the kitchen. "Instant or regular. I never have." He wraps leftover tacos, one at a time, for the kids' lunches. I deposit the plates in the dishwasher and decant the pudding into a clear storage bowl. "What have I done that's so wrong?" he asks.

I take over making the lunches, polishing apples and dropping packs of raisins in each bag. Miranda will forget to take hers and have to borrow money, and Phin won't be seen carrying a lunch bag.

"It's a bowl of chocolate pudding, for Chrissakes." Dan is unable to get off the subject. "Who gives a good goddamn?"

We crash into each other in the narrow part of the kitchen and I drop the bowl. The pudding hits the floor with a slap. We watch the viscid mixture quiver on the white linoleum. The bowl is still rattling under the center island as I leave the kitchen.

"Who's going to clean up the pudding?" Dan calls after me. "If you think it's me, the answer's *like hell I am.*" I head up the stairs. "Well?" I won't answer. "Fine, let it grow legs and walk out on its own."

I close the door of the study. Dan goes out on the deck to smoke.

Pulling up to our house, an expanded Cape Cod in Edgemoor, fills me with deep satisfaction. Especially now while it's still light when I come home from work. Dan's left the Caravan in the driveway instead of pulling into the garage, so I park the Volvo on the street and sit and take in our yard for a little while. The tulips we planted in October are up—the Lilac Perfections, the Burgundy Lace—and Anastasia's paper whites are doing well by the boxwood.

I hear someone playing the piano as I stroll up the front walk. Through the kitchen window I see the table set for dinner with the Bennington pottery, and Dan is cooking. He is an excellent cook. I can handle everyday fare: spaghetti sauce, omelets, tacos, possibly stir-fry. But Dan is as good as any chef. He never follows a recipe and everything is always beautifully presented. He once made red snapper in a thin potato blanket with a Grand Marnier glaze and orange-peel rosettes. Of course, the kids wouldn't touch it.

On the porch, I pull a tiny weed from the oak barrel in which I planted daisies and creeping phlox. "A weed is anything *you* didn't plant," my mother used to say. The phlox has finally begun to spill over the sides and the daisies are a brilliant white.

It's Miranda who's banging on the piano. She plays everything *pesante*—this time *"Für Elise"*—even though her teacher penciled *Lightly!* across the top of the piece. Miranda practices constantly. She plods through scales and pounds out pieces, one hand at a time, for days before she puts them together. I admire the diligence, but she will never be the virtuoso she wants to be or the virtuoso that Phin is. Phin went from lesson to lesson without practicing until he quit last year, but he intuitively understands music. Miranda stomps through Schubert like a storm trooper.

"Hi, sweetheart," I say.

"Shh." She pushes back the skinny braid that hangs down the middle of her forehead to her chin and unconsciously fiddles with the ring in her pierced lower lip.

In the family room, Anastasia is rolling out homemade pink play dough and cutting stars and trees with cookie cutters. She presses down on a cutter with two hands, carefully peels the stars and trees off the table, and holds them up to the light to admire. Red food coloring from the mixture is speckled all the way up her arms and around her mouth.

"Anastasia, honey," I say. "Don't eat the dough." I get a diet ginger ale from the fridge, leaning over the pudding on the floor which, after the month it's been there, has dried and settled into the shape of Bosnia.

I see Dan's spreading canned mushrooms and black olives over a frozen pizza. "It's fine," he says, though I've said nothing. "They like it and it's balanced and I just got home myself."

The piano playing stops and we hear the loud thump of a head being pushed into the wall. Dan and I race for the living room to find out who's assaulting whom.

"You stupid ugly bitch!" Phin yells at Miranda.

"Dammit," Dan says. "Can't you two ever work things out reasonably?"

"She shoved my head into the fucking wall," Phin says.

Dan tells Phin to watch his language and I tell Miranda not to push people's heads into walls. Miranda screams at me for siding with Phin all the time and not even bothering to ask what happened and then says she pushed Phin's head into the wall because he punched her in the back. Phin says he punched her in the back because she karate-chopped him on the neck for flicking her lip ring with his finger. I tell Phin not to touch that lip ring because of the risk of infection, and then I tell Miranda we don't work things out with violence, we negotiate and solve disputes with words. I then suggest Phin and Miranda sit down at the piano and play a nice duet while we're waiting for dinner.

As I leave to change out of my suit, Phin has said or done something to make Miranda angry again and she slaps him.

"Miranda," I say.

"He molested me!" she hollers.

"You wish," Phin says calmly, and flops on the couch with *The New Republic.*

"He sexually harassed me!"

"Shut the fuck up," Phin says. "Make her shut the fuck up," Phin calls to me.

"No means no!" she cries. "No means no!"

"A little bit of peace. Please!" I yell from the stairs, and flatten my hands against my ears.

"What did you say to me?" Miranda threatens her brother, who is eighteen months younger than she. Phin has the gift of words. Well read for a boy his age, he tackled Kafka at eleven, the Russians at thirteen, and he's now struggling on his own with Pynchon. Miranda races up the stairs, crying, and slams the door to her room.

"Let her miss dinner," Dan says, when I return to the kitchen. "She doesn't want to come to the table, she doesn't eat."

"Dinner is family time." I ask Anastasia to please wash up. There's red food coloring smudged all over the table and down the front of her T-shirt. I go upstairs to Miranda's room. "Miranda, honey." I tap on the door. "Please come down for dinner."

"Not with *him* there!" she yells. "And not with you defending him."

"Where do you think you're going?" Dan asks Phin from the front door. Phin's halfway down the lawn already. His girlfriend, who is sixteen, gum-snapping, and futureless, is waiting in her Firebird.

"We were supposed to eat at six," Phin says. "It is now seven. I have plans."

"On a school night?" Dan knows this won't fly with Phin, who has a 3.9 in the gifted program at the Lowery School. "What the hell do those two do every night?" Dan asks, as Phin and Sheryl or Charmin or whatever the girl's name is screech off down our street.

"You don't think she lets him drive, do you?" I ask. Dan looks at me like I've slept through the entire century.

"The leasing company wants to change the loss payee, whatever the hell that is, or something." Dan is slicing pizza with a round cutter.

"I'll call them." I'm trying to hurry Anastasia along at the sink. She's on her footstool holding her hands under the tap.

"I've got to fly to Columbus for a workshop, and the Caravan needs to go for inspection," Dan says.

"I'll drive it to work. I'll get it inspected on the way."

"I'd do it if I could." Dan's voice tightens. "I have to make this workshop."

"I said I'd do it."

"It was the *way* you said you'd do it," he mutters.

"*How* did I say I'd do it?" I am aware of the turn this discussion has taken but unable to stop it.

"You know how you can be," Dan says.

"No, I only know how *you* can get." I pour Ivory Liquid on Anastasia's hands. She lets out an earsplitting scream and starts to cry. To my horror, I see I've poured soap into a multitude of little cuts all over her hands. Dan rushes over to the table where Anastasia was making cookies.

"The cookie cutters," he says, horrified. She'd been slicing up her hands on the sharp edges.

I pull open the drawer by the sink and take out two old cloth diapers, wrap one around each of her hands, and tie off the ends. Dan examines the edges of the cookie cutters for rust. When I return to the kitchen with Neosporin, Anastasia's exactly how I left her, standing on her stool, holding up her hands wrapped in big diaper gloves like a miniature boxer.

"No rust," Dan says. "When was her last tetanus?"

"February. It's a kitchen accident. She wouldn't need a tetanus."

Miranda appears at the kitchen door, her eyes and nose

puffy and red. "What happened?" Her voice is muddy with mucus from crying.

"Daddy let Anastasia play with dangerous cookie cutters." I bandage Anastasia's pinky with gauze.

Dan slips two pieces of pizza off the center island cutting board and storms down to the rec room to watch Jim Lehrer, mozzarella flapping like streamers from his plate. Miranda serves herself some salad, no dressing, and retreats to her room.

"Anastasia," I whisper, eating salad over the sink. "No, no, no, no, no." I shake my finger. She's crouched down, feeling the hard surface of the pudding that's formed. It's difficult to blame her. The top of the pudding is smooth and cool like marble, something children love to touch.

Sometimes when I'm lying in bed, kept awake by Dan's difficult breathing (a deviated septum from breaking his nose in a pickup football game), I wonder if he's ever been unfaithful to me. Whenever I wonder if Dan has made love to another woman, I comfort myself by remembering the belly-button incident, the time Dan couldn't find the navel on a beautiful girl in our infant-and-child first-aid course at the Red Cross. And then I think of Scott, the young man who found mine.

"Find the belly button, people, and place your fist above like so and push in and up like so." Our instructor, Donna, explained the Heimlich maneuver, then grunted like she was being rolfed.

We broke into twos. Dan was paired with a nursing student whose sparkly pink lipstick matched her sweater and socks. I was assigned to Scott, a thirty-year-old broker at Merrill Lynch whose wife was expecting but was on bed rest for toxemia. I played the victim.

"Okay, victims." Donna clapped her hands. "Start coughing. Now choke. Choke! Rescuers, what do you say?"

"Are you all right? Are you all right?" The rescuers asked in unison. "I can help."

Scott moved behind me, placed a hand on my waist, and slid his other hand around, finding my navel with his finger. Then he formed a fist, wrapped his other hand around it, and gently pulled me back. I leaned into him, surprised to feel blood fill my legs, my breasts, rising in my face, blood that had been freeze-dried into a block somewhere behind my navel.

"There's that chicken bone," he whispered in my ear.

"You saved me," I said. While we waited for the teacher to review our work, he rested his chin on my shoulder and kept holding me as I strained to pull my stomach in. He smelled like fresh laundry.

"Excellent work," the instructor commended Scott, and the class applauded. Scott bowed and deferred to me and we sat with the rest of the class, everyone but Dan and the nursing student. The girl was flushed as pink as her lipstick and giggling as Dan fumbled and prodded and missed again and again. Too low or too high, Dan couldn't find the girl's navel. He was so low on one try she had to move his hand away from her crotch. The class howled. Dan was laughing too at this point, shaking his head at himself, looking at the ceiling wondering why a man his age couldn't find the belly button on a beautiful girl. Finally the instructor guided his hand. Then he made a fist and squeezed the girl so hard she yelped like a squeaky toy.

"Hey, you were really good," Scott said, as we left the building and crossed the parking lot.

I tried to think of something smart to say, something like "Choking is my specialty," but tensed as I always do and could only come up with "Thanks, you were good too."

He raised one side of his mouth and cocked his head. "Not really. I just did what the teacher said." He slid his hands into his pockets and squeezed his arms together to wrap his over-sized wool coat more tightly around him. "I guess the true test is what you'll do in a real emergency, isn't it? I worry about that. Whether I'll be able to remember what we learned."

"Of course you're worried." I suddenly relaxed with this young man who left his soap smell on my blouse. "But you'd be surprised at what you remember. It'll be second nature for you." Our walking slowed. Dan had to stop every few yards to wait for us.

"It's a dangerous game, having children," Scott said quietly. We faced each other. He looked at the ground and drew in the gravel with his toe, close to my feet. Dan leaned against our car and lit a cigarette.

"I'm surprised you know that already," I said.

"Yeah, well," he said modestly, and looked at me. "You did really good."

"You too."

Driving home, Dan said, "I think young Mr. Heimlich has a crush on you."

"He's an expectant father." I was trying hard to sound irritated by what Dan had said. "You love the whole world when you're expecting."

"Why couldn't you have married somebody handsome, Jane?" Miranda asks. "Why couldn't you have married somebody like him?" Miranda points to an actor on the sitcom we're watching. Miranda doesn't think she's beautiful regardless of what I tell her. She blames me for marrying her father and fouling up the gene pool. I never considered myself beautiful. I was so clumsy and shy in high school. Miranda disagrees and studies my high school yearbook. "Why'd you go with that geek? You could have gone with the quarterback, or him, or him, or him, or him." She points out boys to whom I was invisible. She picks men on the street I should have married. Also in cars, in stores, in movies. She once rented a movie starring Pierce Brosnan. "That's who you should have married." I told her Pierce Brosnan wasn't available when I was looking for a husband. Besides, I fell in love with her father. Didn't it ever occur to her she wouldn't exist if I had married Pierce Brosnan? "But imagine how cute I'd be," she said.

"What about him, Jane?" she asks. We're watching a show about a handsome single dad whose wife left the family to join a cult. Miranda calls me Jane and makes a point of saying my name in every sentence as though she's trying to beat the Mom out of herself. That way it'll be second nature when her friends are over. Her lip's been bothering her. She keeps turning the ring no matter how much I tell her to leave it alone. She puffs up her cheeks and blows the braid out of her eyes; then she sits back against the couch and tugs on the lip ring.

Pudding

"I'm done, Jane," Mary, our housekeeper, calls to me on her way out. "I still need to get under the fridge, but I can't really with the pudding there. I did clean *around* the pudding." Mary's dying for information about the pudding. I've told her not to touch it, to wax around it. And that's what she's done. The wax has mixed with the pudding at the edges and formed a brown acrylic halo.

I imagined sleeping with Scott. He'd call and want to finish our discussion from after class. We'd meet at the mall across from Merrill Lynch so he could buy a wallpaper border for the baby's room. Could I help him choose? With his wife on bed rest he was left with putting the baby's room together by himself. We'd split a sundae, leaving a thin wall of frozen yogurt where our spoons would otherwise have to touch. Then we'd wind our way up the gradual incline of shops that snake around the mall in a spiral beehive toward the hotel on the top floor, against the traffic of skateboarders, who have found a marble heaven in the winding floors and ramps. Passing the paper store where Dan and I picked the birth announcements for each of our children, the sporting goods store where Phin got his lacrosse equipment, Miranda's favorite record store, we'd float blissfully upward. . . .

At the next class we practiced CPR on dummy babies that lay waiting for us in their own open suitcases, wearing little red and white rompers, scoops for eyes, round holes for mouths, no nostrils. Dan picked his up. "Mama," he made the dummy say, and stretched out its scrawny arms. Dan had become the class favorite, and everybody laughed at his ventriloquist act. When Scott arrived I felt myself flush and saw

Dan smile ironically. Scott nodded at me as he rushed into class late but then paled when he saw his dummy at the front of the room. He lowered himself to his knees and looked into the case, then awkwardly tried to lift the dummy without disturbing its eternal sleep. Donna instructed the class to lay the babies across our desktops and tilt their heads back. Dan made his do the backstroke. Scott never stopped supporting the baby's head.

On the final exam I did well. Dan did better; in fact, he looked like he'd been an emergency medical doctor all his life. He expertly compressed the dummy's chest, gave slow, controlled mouth-to-mouth breaths, checked and rechecked for a pulse every minute. The class applauded enthusiastically at their most popular boy, and Dan saluted the pretty nursing student.

Scott did not do well. He forgot to ask a bystander to call 911. He forgot the number of chest compressions. He never checked for pulse. He left right after the written exam and did not come back for the segment on wounds and burns. Later, Dan and I went out for coffee to celebrate getting the highest scores. I felt rejuvenated with Dan, surprised I'd given someone else a second thought.

By now Scott's had his baby, perhaps even another, and he and his wife are getting up to speed with the rest of us.

Someone has stamped out a cigarette in the pudding. I call Phin downstairs to see what he knows. *"I didn't put a cigarette in the pudding!"* he shouts in my face, nearly scaring me to death.

"Maybe one of your friends or Sheryl—"

Pudding

"None of my friends put a cigarette in the pudding!"

"All right, Phin," I say softly. "It could have been the housekeeper."

Miranda has appeared at the kitchen door. "I'm cleaning up the pudding." She's holding a bucket and a bundle of old cloth diapers that we now use as rags. "I can't stand it anymore."

"Because you're embarrassed in front of your friends?" I ask.

"I'm cleaning it up."

"Oh, no, you're not, young lady." I walk away. Miranda drops the bucket and rags and runs upstairs.

"I bet if Phin wanted to clean up the pudding you'd let him," she shrieks from her room.

I take Phin to the doctor to find out why he's "itching and burning in a place guys don't like to itch and burn." He has a flaming case of gonorrhea. Driving home he moves uncomfortably in his seat and pretends to be interested in every car we pass.

I take a deep breath. "Phin, do you know about condoms?" I ask my handsome son.

"Yes."

"Do you use them?"

"Yes."

"All the time, Phin?"

"All the time."

"Okay." I feel like I'm going to cry.

Instead of going home I drive to the nature center and pull into the parking lot.

"Remember we came here when you were little?" I ask Phin, and take a space next to a school bus. "Remember? We went sledding and I brought you here to warm up?"

"No."

There's a large group of excited kindergartners outside the building. A teacher and some volunteers are trying to organize them. "Okay, kids. Time to get with your buddies and hold hands," the teacher yells. The kids form two squirmy lines held together by little hands. A volunteer wraps a ribbon around the group, ties a knot, and makes a handle for the teacher to pull.

"That should hold 'em," the volunteer says.

Phin digs his hands deep in the pockets of a maroon-and-white letter jacket stolen from Sheryl's high school as we walk across the lot. The jacket's too big for him. His arms are lost in the leather sleeves.

I'm surprised the nature center hasn't been better maintained or the exhibits updated. Some of the displays I recognize from when I brought Phin here as a three-year-old—mostly Plexiglas boxes with stuffed birds and animals or leaves that you're likely to see in Rock Creek Park. Phin glances over at the park ranger, who's giving a tour to the kindergarten class.

"This ugly orange fungus is called a stinkhorn," the ranger says. The kindergartners laugh at the word. "It's called a stinkhorn because of the unpleasant odor it emits." The kindergartners are beside themselves with laughter.

"Look, Phin, the birds of Washington, D.C." Phin comes over for a look at pigeons behind Plexiglas.

"Now, what's interesting about the stinkhorn," the ranger

says, and Phin looks back over, "is how fast it grows. It's completely developed in just a couple of hours." The kids are perplexed by this information.

"Phin, look at all the different kinds of spider webs," I say.

"Flies eat the spores on top," the ranger says, pointing to a picture of the strange fungus, which looks like an orange rhinoceros horn. "And the spores stick to the flies." The kids have their mouths hanging open, and so does Phin. He's let the sleeves of the jacket fall down over his hands like flippers. "And flies spread the fungi all through the forest." There's total quiet for a moment; then a boy in the back of the line says "Stinkhorn," breaking the spell. The class laughs and moves on to the Birds of Washington, D.C.

"Isn't that interesting," I say in front of a squirrel display. "I never knew the black squirrel was a color phase of the gray squirrel."

"Yes, you did." Phin is looking at the stuffed raccoon.

"No, I really didn't."

Phin slides his fingers over the raccoon's box, enjoying the smoothness of the Plexiglas. "They had those same squirrels when we came here before. And you said the same thing then."

I can't sleep. My son has gonorrhea, Miranda loathes herself, and Anastasia is three and has barely begun talking. I go down to the kitchen for a mug of warm milk and see a little chocolate footprint in the middle of the pudding. The crust has broken through to the soft custard, still velvety after all these months. I follow a trail of fading chocolate feet to Anastasia's bedroom and watch her sleep in her deathlike way, not moving, hardly breathing. Miranda used to sleep this way too. Once or twice I shook her awake to make sure she was alive. . . .

Someone calls "Mom!" and I wake up with a start. The voice is too old for Anastasia.

"Mom!" Miranda calls from her bedroom.

I jump up, tearing my gown on a protruding nail at the base of our platform bed, and cross the hall to Miranda's room. Her lip is puffed up three sizes and curled over the ring completely. I touch it. It's hard as cement and she's obviously in terrible pain. "Mommy," she says. I get her up and dressed. She lets me pull her camisole over her head and dress her in a pair of leggings, an oversized New York Knicks T-shirt, and her blue boat decks. I hold her hand and lead her out of her room.

"What's going on here?" Dan looks out from the dark bedroom, squinting from the light in the hall.

"I'm taking Miranda to the emergency room."

A resident who looks like he could use some sleep studies Miranda's lip, trying to figure out what to do. I imagine they didn't cover lip rings in med school. "Yep," he says, "we're definitely going to have to get that ring outa there." Miranda starts to cry. I lean over her on the gurney and hug her shoulders. I tell her it's going to be fine. I'll hold her the entire time; there won't be a scar. The resident injects her chin with a nerve block, and as soon as she loses feeling he goes to work with a tiny pair of wire clippers.

"It's going really well." I lie to Miranda and squeeze her hand. There's a lot of blood and I feel like killing the resident.

"When was her last tetanus?" the resident asks, trying to snip the ring with the clippers.

"She had a booster two years ago February."

The resident steps back and lets the nurse, a short man with ridiculously huge biceps, dab the blood off her chin.

"So, Miranda." The resident tries to distract her. "You're a Knicks fan?"

"No," Miranda says, her eyes darting around the emergency room. "The shirt's just my way of saying thank you to New York for sending Pat Riley to the Heat."

The resident and nurse think this is great and laugh. The nurse pats her knee. I didn't know Miranda knew anything about basketball.

"Aren't you a Washington Bullets—excuse me, Wizards—fan?" I ask.

"Trade Webber for Mourning and I'll be a Wizards fan," she says. "And lose Bickerstaff. He's as bad as Unseld."

"Hold on," the nurse says. "Wes Unseld is my man."

"Great player, a coaching disaster," Miranda says.

I don't know what any of these people are talking about. There's a loud snip, and I'm certain the resident's cut right through her lip, there's so much blood, but then he holds up the bloody ring in the tweezers. *Voilà.*

At home we find the whole family in bed. Dan and Anastasia are curled together and Phin is lying at the foot with the remote control, watching an old black-and-white movie. When he realizes we're there he flips to a hockey game rebroadcast on ESPN. Miranda flops next to him and tries to grab the remote control, which he holds up over her head. Anastasia and Dan sleep through the racket. Phin reaches over to touch the little Band-Aid on Miranda's lip and she slaps his hand. He tries again, slowly and softly this time, and she lets him press around her swollen bottom lip, proud of her wound. She knows she's impressed him.

I hate to break up such a rare time, but it's late so I shoo them off to their rooms. Anastasia and Dan are so nicely curled together, I let her stay the night.

In the morning, I cut a deal with Dan. If he'll agree to chip the pudding off the linoleum with an ice pick, I'll sweep the pieces. The pudding chips off easier than we imagined and I sweep it effortlessly into the dustpan. Dan goes a step beyond the agreement and Spic & Spans the area with the sponge mop until the floor sparkles. Then we stand in our kitchen and drink fresh coffee and admire the house we've put so much work into. Anastasia's at ballet. Phin's at soccer. Miranda's gone for a walk with her friend. Everything is calm. It's a beautiful morning in October: the leaves at peak, the air refreshing. Our kitchen floor is as clean and white as glacier ice on a bright arctic day.

"So," Dan says.

"So," I say, which is exactly what we said after our first date in college, when Dan walked me to the door of my basement apartment in Georgetown, battling back the wisteria that had overgrown the steps to my studio, slicing through the vines, our arms like machetes, to get to my bed. Only then it was clear he was coming in for the night. Now we have the whole glorious morning to ourselves and don't quite know what to do.

Lives of the Invertebrates

I'd never seen one so big, dead or alive. I take clients to steak houses in Boston, Philly, San Francisco, and Dallas; the husbands get steak; the wives casually pick at the magnificent lobsters from Nova Scotia, their tremendous claws quiet above their heads on the platter like the gloved hands of a fallen champ. But even those are generally no more than three-pounders.

I was skimming my *Barron's,* strolling down a corridor at Logan, not in any particular hurry to catch my shuttle home, when I saw him. A hastily written sign on a white paper plate with fluted edges, duct-taped to a Popsicle stick, read, MEET MAX! THE EIGHT-POUND LOBSTER! I wondered, as I moved

JULIA SLAVIN

over to the tank, how old a lobster would have to be to get that big. Forty maybe. My age.

He took up half the tank. A détente appeared to have been invoked, perhaps a respect for age and relative misfortune, from the one- and one-and-a-half-pounders, who stayed pressed over on the other side of the tank. A couple of the one-pounders were scrapping it out, their claws bound tight by thick blue bands. They took turns jabbing at each other with their neutered claws for nonexistent territory in their final act before clutching each other in the bottom of a steamer pot. Except for his antennae, which swayed with the waves created by the boxing one-pounders, Max barely moved. Occasionally he'd raise a massive claw, as though he were going to rise up out of his situation. But then he'd give up and let it float down to the steel bottom of the tank. I wondered if perhaps he was sick. More likely he was exhausted after his journey from Canada. Or maybe he just didn't have the stuff for a fight anymore. His eyes were hard to locate amid his massive blue-mottled shell, and I know now that lobsters don't really see, that they rely on vibration and feel with their antennae, but I swear he was looking at me.

"You're not going to sell him," I said to the guy behind the tank, with a name tag that read CARL.

" 'Course we're going to sell him." Carl blew smoke out of his nostrils and surveyed a crowd of flight attendants rushing by, a school of navy blue fish, with their neat bags on little wheels, the fabric of their pants stretching tight with each step.

"A lobster that big must be forty years old, maybe more," I said. "It doesn't seem right to end that way."

"I dunno," Carl said. "I don't usually work over here. Hey, Deucah!" he called, to a maintenance man passing by.

The man came over. They hit fists and exchanged separate salvos of "No fuckin' way" and "Ya fuckin' kiddin' me?" and "Get da fuck outa here." I always wonder where airport workers come from. Do they live nearby? Airports are so far away from everything. It's not like you can go out to lunch or forget a document at home and rush back. You're stuck. But watching Carl suck his lips at everything that went by in a skirt and push smoke out of his unfriendly face like the back of a bus, it was probably better to keep him marooned.

I leaned against a cement pillar across the corridor and tried to read my paper. But I couldn't stop looking over at Max. He looked so sad. I was startled by a hand on my arm. A short woman, twenty-five maybe, looked up at me. "You're right about that lobster," she said. "It's inhumane. I'm a vegan myself."

I nodded, then noticed her looking at my hand to see if I had a ring and clenched my jaw to keep from asking her if she wanted a cup of coffee, or for her phone number. I saw the satisfied smile of my therapist. "Getting involved with a woman at the airport. Perfect," he'd say, tapping his fingers on the teak coffee table that my twelve years of therapy helped to finance. "She'll fly off and you'll never see her again." The woman could tell by my polite smile, and the silent language that single people speak to one another, that we weren't going anywhere. She said good luck and walked off with her Le Sportsac. Who knows? Maybe she was the one. Probably not.

I have a history of getting involved with women who dump

me or cheat on me, the most non-dumping non-cheating women in the world. Sweet women that I somehow drive away, my therapist says. Women named Wendy and Mary and Virginia, loving, smart, nurturing women, marrying types. There was even a girl cruelly misnamed Faith who went to bed with her paralegal the night before our engagement party. She said I was suffocating her. Wendy called me an octopus. Mary said she couldn't turn around without an arm around her, a hand on every inch of her exemplary little body, that I was sucking the life out of her.

I admit I'm aggressive. It's worked well for me in business. At twenty-nine, I was the youngest chief financial officer in my company's history. But my success in business has worked in inverse proportion with my personal life. I love women. I want to marry them. I want to make them happy. I can't leave them alone. I can't stop calling them and asking where they've been. When I'm upset with them, I don't play coy or distant. I come right out and ask who they've been with and why they haven't called. What I consider zeal, women deem strangulation. My therapist claims it's what I intend all along: for them to leave me. "All you really want," he says, "is to be alone." I don't buy it. I find a tuna fish sandwich in front of C-SPAN at ten o'clock every night to be a very lonely sandwich.

"You gonna buy him?" Carl asked, after I'd moved back over to the tank, as if caught in an undertow. " 'Cause there was a guy here before, a Texan guy, wanting to buy him. Said he'd be back after a drink." I knew Carl was lying, but he was right. If anyone was going to buy the lobster, it would be a Texan. I do a lot of business with Texans. They get more

Texan when they're out of Texas. He'd buy it for his peroxided wife. And then show it off in the Admirals Lounge.

"Yeah, I want him," I said, feeling the excitement of not knowing what I was going to do next.

Carl slid off the top of the tank. I heard the loud gurgling of the air pump. Then he produced a huge pair of forceps and grasped the lobster around the head. It started to bend and twist at the middle. The tank clouded. Water splashed out and wet Carl's pants. "Fuck!" he yelled, and lifted the forceps over his head like he was going to stab something.

"Careful!" I shouted. He plunged the forceps back into the water and managed to get a grip around the lobster's middle. It went limp. He lifted it out. Max spread his claws. There must have been a three-foot span. I was amazed.

"Looka that," Carl said. "Hey, Scoopy," he called to an airport worker who was pushing an empty wheelchair down the corridor. "P'seidon. King a da sea." Then he dumped Max in a plastic-lined cardboard carrying box like he was trash.

I paid him sixty-five dollars and looked around for some seaweed or something to put in the box with Max so it wouldn't be quite so inhospitable. But there were only lobster bibs and jars of cocktail sauce at the stand. I went to the gift shop and bought a Celtics T-shirt to put him on. At the counter, I opened the box. A claw raised up out of the top and flopped down on the side. The clerk jumped back.

"It's okay," I said. "He's got bands around his claws. He can't hurt you."

"Oh." She laughed, embarrassed. "I've just never seen one so big."

"You gonna steam him or broil him?" the customer behind me asked.

"No, I'm not eating him. I'm taking him to an aquarium," I said, surprising myself. This had just occurred to me, and I thought it was an excellent idea.

"I like 'em broiled," the man said, ignoring my answer. "With *buttah*. But remember, you have to cut that vein on the neck while's they're alive. Then cut 'em down the middle so's they lie flat. One that big I'd steam."

"Thanks for the tip," I said. Moron.

I called the Boston aquarium. They told me to call the zoo. I called the zoo. They told me they'd transfer me to the invertebrate house. "It's a lobster, not a snake," I said to the woman on the phone, who, because of her thick Boston accent, I took, wrongly, as an idiot.

"A lobstah is an invertebrate, sir," she said. "A snake is a reptile."

"Oh."

"We already have a lobster," the woman at the invertebrate house said.

"Can't you take another?" I asked, holding the phone to my ear with my shoulder, my case of documents weighing down one hand, the lobster box weighing down the other.

"We have to fight to keep the one we have," she said sadly. "They're not considered unusual enough. Especially here. If you had a cuttlefish, or a Portuguese man-of-war . . ."

I walked through the airport feeling dejected. I'd missed the three-thirty and the four would be boarding soon. The lobster shifted his weight in the box. I put my documents down and gently tilted the box back so he was centered. I was heading for the gate when I heard the page. "Would the man with the lobster go to one of the gray courtesy phones." A group of lawyers I recognized from taking the shuttle all the time laughed, and so did everyone else in the waiting area when the page was repeated.

"Sorry about the page," the woman from the invertebrate house said. "I didn't know your name."

"Never mind," I said. "You're a doll."

"Washington's lobster died. They might be looking for a new one."

Three voices later I was on with Katherine Crisp in Washington, Associate Keeper of Invertebrates. Katherine had a voice that went through me like heavy syrup. I can tell a lot from voices since I spend so much time on the phone. "You see," she said, low and unwavering, "it's not up to me. It's up to the zoo constable." A slight sexy lisp on *constable.*

"The zoo constable," I repeated. I shifted my weight, trying not to become distracted by the movement I felt behind my fly. "May I speak with the zoo constable?" I asked.

"The constable is a board," she said. "The board meets the second Tuesday of every even month." It was July. I remembered what I hated so much about Washington, the city in a swamp, why I avoid business there. No one's individually accountable: it's always boards or committees or, worse, policy. "And it was the decision of the board not to replace the lobster."

"Too common?" I said, getting angry.

"If it were up to me . . ." The city's anthem. But I kept

cool. There was a person on the other end of the line, a person who saw the world from her own personal vantage point. How could we both come out ahead?

"Okay," I said. "I see a display. Mighty Max the lobster, rescued on his way to becoming Thermidor." That got a throaty hum of a laugh. "And the sign goes on to say that a lobster this big is this old and would you want to eat a lobster this old?" I'd botched it, I knew.

"We're not anti-seafood," Katherine said. "In fact we have a display of spices and hot sauces."

"I guess if it were a cuttlefish you'd feel different." I was losing ground, if I had to go the self-pitying route.

"Cuttlefish change color and pattern when they're threatened," she purred. "Big hit with the kids." Sometimes the best negotiating tactic is to keep quiet. Let your counterpart wriggle around with words and pauses. Let her spar it out by herself and come to what *you* believe on her own. "I mean, this is a zoo, not a shelter," she said, after several quiet moments. "Are you still there?"

"I'm here." I was closing in for the kill.

"I could suggest you take it back to the ocean," she said. Silence. "But of course we both know what would eventually happen to it anyway." Done deal. "Can you bring him down to D.C.?"

"I'm at an airport," I said triumphantly. "I can get him to Timbuktu."

As soon as the flight attendant buckled herself in I took the box out from under the seat and held it. Max moved gently on my lap, shadowing the rocking motion of the plane, on his way to salvation. But as I drifted off to sleep, the last thing I remember thinking about was Katherine. And I said it aloud to test it: "Katherine, Katherine."

She didn't look like what I'd imagined. Do they ever? I always imagine, and I'm not proud of this, but it's what comes to mind, that they look like Veronica from Archie comics. Brown wavy hair and a ridiculous hourglass body with big pointed breasts. I said I wasn't proud of the image.

Katherine had brown hair but it was short, short-short, high above her ears, which were small and lobeless. Something simple, she'd told her hairdresser. No jewelry. No excess. A few light freckles were sprinkled across her nose and cheeks, faded from lack of sun, from working all day in near darkness, and her skin was so white she looked like she was standing under fluorescents. She was thin. So thin. Tiny breasts, if any at all. Dressed in the uniform of the other zookeepers, male and female, green polo shirt and navy khakis, she could easily be mistaken for a boy.

I saw her by the anemone tank, explaining something to a zoo volunteer. A tremendous pink anemone sucked on the glass just above her head. She curled her lip at something the volunteer said, then quickly closed her mouth when she looked at me and noticed I saw she wore braces. I was shocked by them. I wonder about grown-ups who get braces. Why did they wait? Was it the money? Were they too vain? Did they have an accident? In a practiced way, she spoke with her lips out and over her teeth to cover the braces and managed to talk without revealing them.

"You're the man with the lobster?" she called over the volunteer's shoulder.

"That's me," I said. She didn't smile. Maybe her smile was on hiatus while the braces were on. Maybe I'd be the one to bring it back.

"I'll be with you shortly," she said.

The invertebrate house was nearly empty, most of the kids preferring lions and gorillas, animals that really look like animals. I stood by the sponge display while she signed some papers for the volunteer. I remember it was a big deal to have a real sponge in the bath or by the sink when I was growing up. They seemed to multiply in our house. I always found it rather disgusting, using an animal to wash yourself.

Katherine motioned for me to follow her to the back. "I hope your coming wasn't in vain," she said. "I still need the okay from the constable. Not to mention the space." I watched her back, straight and rigid, as we walked. We passed the octopus display. I was relieved to read a sign that said they didn't really sink ships or eat people, that they're really quite timid and keep to themselves.

"Ah, my nemesis," I said as we passed the cuttlefish, who was, at the moment, beige. He clearly had the best tank, the prime real estate.

"We're getting another in September," Katherine said proudly.

We passed an empty tank where the old lobster had lived. There were still rocks and sediment at the bottom. It looked like a nice place for my lobster to make his residence. Katherine saw my hopeful gaze. "Sorry. That's for the new cuttlefish."

She took me back to a large lab and storage area. Metal

tubs lined the wall. Siphons, jars of pebbles, old pumps, trow-els, and boxes of crystallized chemicals were piled on shelves. The middle of the room was taken up by a huge round Jacuzzi-looking tank where two horseshoe crabs lived. All this for a couple of horseshoe crabs. I remember as a kid there were always a couple of dead horseshoe crabs on the beach at Riis Park after a full moon, a few of the unfortunate ones that came to the shore to mate and couldn't make their way back home. I'd included them with the wrappers, plastic cups, driftwood, and condoms that washed up on the beach, certainly not worthy of a tank at the zoo.

"Why are they back here?" I asked.

"For demonstrations. For kids." She sank her bare arms into the water and picked up one of the crabs. "This is Es-ther." Water dripped off her thin arms. "One of the last sur-viving cousins of the trilobites. A relic from 250 million years ago."

She turned the crab over and stroked her underside. Es-ther's legs stopped moving and she became still; bubbles formed at her mouth, or what I assumed was her mouth. "Look at that eye," Katherine said, turning Esther back onto her stomach. "The most sophisticated eye in the universe." It looked like a dot to me, like my lobster's eye. "She lives in the mud but can see everything. Watch."

She lowered Esther back into the tank, crossed to the other side, and dropped in a small freeze-dried shrimp. Esther rose from the bottom and glided over. The shrimp disappeared under her shell and Esther sank down into the sludge. Katherine dropped in more shrimp, and another horseshoe crab appeared, which Katherine introduced as Sadie. Then she turned to one of the worktables where I'd put down my box.

"Let me." I reached to take over, but she waved me off. Her hands disappeared in the box. She lifted Max. He went limp in her hands. "He likes you," I said, relieved.

"She," Katherine corrected, and turned Max over on the damp Celtics shirt. "Eggs," she said, stroking a dark area around the abdomen. "Or, as they say in the restaurant business, roe."

"How old would you say he is?" I asked. "I mean she."

Katherine shrugged. "Sixty. Sixty-five. Seventy." I was stunned. "She's going to be fine," Katherine said, keeping her eyes focused on the lobster, swaddled in the green receiving blanket. "We'll find a place for her. Either here or at another zoo. She won't go to a restaurant."

I felt all the stress of the day wash out of me.

"What did you name her?" Katherine asked, stroking her tail.

Now that I'd saved her I felt I *could* name her, my own name, not the name that heinous Carl at the airport had stuck her with. "Gina," I said. I don't know where I got that. I guess it sounded like Regina, my family's cleaning lady. The one who used real sponges to get the floors clean. I always liked her. "Gina," I said again.

"She's beautiful, all right," Katherine said. I felt proud. "I've never seen such a large crusher," she said, shaking hands with Gina's heavier claw. "Strong pincers." Her tongue caught on her braces and she lisped: *pintherth.* I found it too sexy for words. I asked her to dinner.

She pulled some garlands of seaweed out of a freezer and made an underwater nest on one side of the tank and positioned some large rocks. Then she lowered Gina into the tank. "They'll keep to themselves," Katherine said, and dropped in more frozen shrimp.

As we walked into the hazy July evening, we shielded our eyes from the light, our pupils the size of dimes from being in the dark. "It must be fun to work in the dark all day," I said. "It must be cozy." Katherine pulled a pair of Jackie O sunglasses from her day pack, the only accessory she allowed herself. I thought she looked elegant. Her pale skin and skinny body began to look almost fashionable in her zoo uniform.

We looked up and down Connecticut Avenue. I didn't know where to take her for dinner. Certainly not a place with shellfish. And there were all those foods that could get stuck in her braces and embarrass her. She chose a place with coal-oven pizza, which she ate in tiny bites with a fork, carefully opening her lips, out and over the braces, pursing them down on the tines. She kept catching me staring at her mouth. I wanted to see the braces. I wanted to know what was wrong with her teeth.

"You know, I never liked zoos much when I was a kid," she said, pushing her plate back and folding her hands on the table. She'd eaten one piece without the crust. I was faced with five more slices of our large plain pizza.

"I can't imagine a little girl not liking the zoo," I said. But I could imagine Katherine. A pale skinny girl in a party dress with crooked teeth. Or maybe they were buck. Buck teeth and braids. That was Katherine, I was certain.

"But I see their value now," she went on. "For young people. To observe and respect animals. If one person can be stopped from throwing plastic into the water, or realize the importance of not cutting down trees or widening roads into the bay, then we've done some good." We gave the rest of the pizza to a guy bumming money outside the restaurant and went back to the zoo.

As we walked through the entrance, past the bat house, the flamingo cage, the okapis, I put my hand on the small of Katherine's back. Her bones poked through like sticks. She moved away. We strolled along not saying anything.

The zoo was oddly quiet, now that the kids had gone and the animals had stopped performing. I begged for two cones from a snow-cone vendor who was closing up, and he gave them to us, no charge. We sat on a bench near the prairie dogs and she crossed her thin legs, the foot of her top leg reaching all the way down to the cement. She bit into her snow cone. "Ouch," she said, and held her hand to her mouth.

"Cold?" I asked, looking at her mouth, hoping for the slightest peek.

"Mmm," she said, giving me nothing.

I kissed her. She kept her mouth closed. I turned my head away and sat back, looking at the sun, which was just setting behind the lions' den. I kissed her again. This time she opened her mouth. I felt her tongue go from cold to warm. Then I started to move my tongue around. I wanted to feel the braces. The hard next to the soft. Steel on velvet. But she protected the precious metal with her tongue and I couldn't get in. We started a pushing match with our tongues. She was winning. I wasn't anywhere near. I put my hand on her breast and felt a hard nipple through her polo shirt. She moved my hand away and stopped kissing me, looking around to make sure no one had seen. I put my hands on her bony shoulders and tried to turn her body toward me but she stood up. She took my hand and we walked back to the invertebrate house, not saying a word.

Back in the invertebrate house, I stood before a cockroach display while Katherine dimmed some lights and raised others.

"Must not have been too hard to put *this* display together," I said, as an icebreaker, but then realized she must hear that one all the time. They were crawling on top of one another. The bugs on the bottom, resigned to being stuck, waiting it out until the bullies went elsewhere. I tried to look at them as nature, as beings that have been here as long as time, but there's no way around it, they're disgusting.

I felt something on my waist behind me. I jumped. "It's just me," Katherine said. She slid her hands around my sides to the top of my belt. I hoped she wasn't going to try to undo my belt or rub her hands over my crotch because I wasn't ready. I'd lost the mood, watching the cockroaches. I started to turn around but she wrapped her arms tightly around me and was smoothing her hands over my chest. She was strong for someone so slight. I tried to pull my stomach in as she brought her hands down over it, tried to improve my posture as she rubbed her face on my spine. Most of all, I tried to remember what I'd found so attractive about her.

"Let's check on Gina," I said.

"Okay," Katherine said, rejection in her voice. She dropped her arms and led the way to the storage room. We passed the cuttlefish. He'd turned red. I put my hand on the back of her neck. My fingers wrapped almost all the way around it. She looked up at me and smiled with her mouth closed. In the storage room, she dimmed lights and hung her keys on a nail by a wall phone. I looked in the tank. Esther glided across the surface and bumped into the side like a plastic float, then wobbled back to the middle. Katherine looked puzzled, her face screwed up. She reached across the tank and touched the crab. Esther bobbed in the water. Katherine bent over the tank, straining at the waist, her shirt coming untucked, and turned over an empty shell.

"My God," she gasped. "The lobster's attacked the crabs." She thrust her arms into the water. "I can't find Sadie," she cried, her arms churning the water into froth. "Sadie's not here. And I can't find the lobster!"

Katherine shimmied around the tank, making white water with her arms. I lowered my arms into the water, drenching my sleeves, almost instinctively to the exact place where Gina had crawled after devouring the crabs. I held her around the middle and raised her up out of the water.

"I have her," I said. "She's fine."

"Sadie's gone," Katherine said, shaking off her arms.

"The crabs must have cut through the rubber bands," I said, looking at Gina's claws, wide open, victorious.

"No," Katherine said, utterly annoyed with me. "They don't bother the large crustaceans. They're shy." She stomped over and glared at Gina, examining her for crab shell or tentacles or *meat*.

Gina, who'd been slack in my hands, suddenly arched the front section of her body back. I tried to get control of her but I couldn't get the right grip. I felt myself start to slip on the wet floor as she lunged toward Katherine, scissoring through her upper lip with her cutter claw like it was paper. I saw a flash of silver gleam in the dim light of the lab and then a gush of red that poured down Katherine's chin like spilled paint. She stumbled backward, lifted her hand to her mouth, touched herself with her fingertips, and looked at the blood on her hand. Gina lunged again and flew out of my hands, landed on the floor with a smack, and crawled around the tank. I grabbed the Celtics T-shirt balled up on a worktable. Katherine snatched it from me and held it to her mouth to stop the blood. I picked up the wall phone and dialed 911. Katherine shook her head, made a grotesque gurgling sound out of her mouth, and pointed to a security number taped to the wall. Then she stepped back and lowered herself to the floor, leaning against the tank. I punched in the numbers and sat down facing her. Our feet touched. She whipped her knees into her chest.

"You know, it's going to be okay," I said, waiting for security to answer. "Everything is going to be all right."

She looked at me for a moment, her pupils like black pearls. Then she pulled the shirt away from her mouth to look at the blood. Red bubbles foamed from her lips.

"Keep it covered," I said. "Keep pressure on it."

But she paid no attention to what I said and never looked at me again. As far as Katherine was concerned, I wasn't there anymore. I was excess. I'd invaded her world like a virus. I should be flushed away with everything unnecessary.

"There's been an accident," I said, when security answered. "In the invertebrate house." Then I saw Gina, by the side of the tank, looking at me. She wanted to know what we were going to do next, where we were going to go, why we were still here. She waited for my answer, unflinching, her eyes locked on mine for what felt like forever.

Blighted

First there was a scratch: a twig blown across the window. Then a thud: a branch thrown against the house. Paint rained down from the ceiling, and plaster hit the floor in a single sheet. A second bash against the house felt like a Cessna missed the airport; I grabbed the maple highboy in the corner and screamed for the neighbors next door. Then it stopped.

I let go of the dresser and looked at the damage to my walls. A fissure in the ceiling now divided the room in two. In the quiet I listened. It was a June night. And still. I peered out the window in search of the mystery assailant, looking up and down, the white oak between my house and the Bradleys' still trembling slightly after the collision.

My God, I thought, it was the oak. And there was the branch that had caused the damage. I put a hand on my hip and shook my finger. "A little trim would do you good." And with that, it reared back, paused to unfurl, and shot forward through the window. Everything went out of focus as I was blinded by shattered glass. Spitting shards and blood, blinking wildly, I saw it rear back again. I tried to dive away but it caught me in an awkward leaf-rustling vise grip, lifted me into the air, and slammed me down on my bed. I managed to lift my head: My legs were free, I could move my arms, but I was pinned. I pushed the branch, hoping to slip out, but a stalk of trumpet creeper caught me around the neck and jerked my head back. I wrapped my fingers between my neck and the vine to make room for little bursts of breathing and started to kick: bicycles, crescent fronts, scissors. But with such little oxygen, my legs soon fell heavy and useless on the bed. I closed my eyes. A leaf tickled my ear. I raised my shoulder to stop it. Another tickle. I was being tickled and grazed and brushed all over, then lapped. Wet leaves all over me. I tasted dirt, felt the puffed-out veins of a leaf on my tongue. Leaves covered my breasts like a bikini top. I felt the tightening of being wrapped in a cradle of bark. My legs were nudged apart now by a two-pronged limb and I was completely exposed, the air rushing in from the broken window. But there was something warm and wet, a rough pointed tip with a felty pubescence underneath. I called out again for the neighbors as best I could with the strangling vine, but at the same time my hips were rising.

When I awoke, half the morning was gone. The covers were pushed down, my nightgown was balled up under my arms. I rolled onto my side and saw the bark sheddings, the leaves that had dropped on my rug and quilt, the broken glass, the damage to my walls and ceiling. A disoriented dove pecked the rug, lifted up, banged against the rear window, and flapped around the floor on its back. I sat up and opened my gown. My body was scraped, rib cage to ankles, as though I'd been dragged under a car. Outside, my oak swayed in a moist wind from the south.

You should know, my next-door neighbor, Del Bradley, built himself a cathedral for a kitchen. It included a gas grill, a wood-burning stove, and a brick pizza oven with vents shooting out the top of a ribbed vault that could be seen for miles around. There were pillars of Purbeck marble and frosted glass and an eight-sided ceiling that Del said was inspired by the octagon of Ely. There were potted palms as high as the roof and indoor window boxes of geraniums. Del's wife, Marguerite, had developed a pathological fear of all places but their home, after her last child left, and Del said if he couldn't get her out he'd bring the outside in. It wasn't long before he started replacing other rooms in his house with chapels and cloisters and arcades that led to spare bedrooms that workers had turned into Sistine masterpieces. For each new room added to the fortress, an old tree was cleared. This week a pair of tulip poplars, delimbed and chopped into block, next a hickory, ground to mush in a chipper, a group of beeches now stacked up behind Del's house for firewood. It seemed wrong, ecologically, to take down a tree for a house. But Del and Marguerite had been good neighbors, through my divorce and all the years of being alone, and I wasn't going to stand in the way. They were apologetic about the noise; I waved them off. They were ashamed of the chemical-shit smell of the outdoor Sanijohn that wafted over on hot summer nights. Nothing I can't live with, I told them, and brought over pots of soup and banana bread while their kitchen was under dust. But then Del came to discuss the oak between us.

"I've tried to work it into our plans, Carla. Hired and fired three landscapers, because you are right, it is an excellent Quercus."

My oak. To be slaughtered for a master bathroom. I shook my head, squeezed my lips into a frown.

Since my first encounter with the tree, a lot of the kinks had been worked out of our activity. I'd covered the window with plastic strips to avoid glass breaking, and there was less sense of urgency. The branch never crashed through the wall anymore but floated in, squeezing its limbs to fit the small space, then growing, stretching, giving the wildlife a chance to pack and flee. Our moments had become tender and slow. Sometimes I'd climb on top, moving knob to burl. Maybe from behind, two limbs across my chest, a cluster of leaves flickering at the backs of my thighs, and then rolling over and under its tremendous, reassuring weight. During the night, as I slept, it would draw back into itself, the leaves kissing against the side of my house. I made a place for myself in the branch with pillows and a folded blanket, and soon thick leaves grew over my perch and I lived in the tree. In the leaves, there were whispers and voices. My mother's voice— nothing extraordinary—playing cards with the women in our town, the sound of money sliding off a table into a hand. My grandparents arguing on a train. There were children. Someone crying up in the crown, the boughs too soft to climb. My father, not a voice but a shadow from a bough, in his wool coat, smiling at me in the last seconds of his life. Between us there were no boundaries.

"The root system, which is extensive," Del went on, "is interfering with our raising the ground." He smoothed his hand through the air above the grass. "It's going to be good, Carla, for both of us. We'll plant new trees between us, a row of hollies, some cedars. More human-level trees."

"All the destruction, Del. It doesn't seem right."

Del looked at the ground between us. He felt bad about what he had to say, I could tell. "It is, after all, lawfully, on my property."

I looked over at the branch. It was nearly four o'clock. It would be reaching out soon. "I can't give you my blessing on this one."

"Now, Carla, you know that Marguerite and I—"

"Have been so good to me."

"I know it's not easy being . . ."

Everything got uncomfortable, as it does when my aloneness is mentioned. Women my age have husbands and grown children. Or they live in the city. Family life never came together for me; a six-month marriage to a policeman who broke my cheekbone and a rib with his fists was as close as I got to having my own family. I let Del wiggle and tick while he tried to think of something to pave over the unease. He shifted foot to foot, rearranged some phlegm in his throat, and then I noticed the branch pushing into the window.

"We'll have to finish this discussion later, Del." I scurried up the path to the house.

"It's all set to go Wednesday, Carla. Tree guys are hard to pin down."

By the time I got upstairs there was a mess of covers and clothes and pulled-out drawers as the branch turned over the room in a blind search. "I'm here, I'm here." I waved my arms to stop it. It then came at me with a thrust so hard the wind was knocked clear out of me. Just like old times.

Other towns have regulations about air rights and building responsibly and more enlightened notions of the ownership of property, but not this town. After searching through some dusty three-ring binders at our town hall, I did manage to find an ordinance from the 1950s about cutting healthy trees, which I Xeroxed and brought back for Del.

"Good of you to take time from your day, Carla." He was concerned, kept shaking his head in disbelief at what he was reading. He lifted his eyes from the paper. "My lord. The poplars. The beeches, the hickory." He looked around like we were under surveillance by police. Del Bradley abided by the law. Never jaywalked. Never drove over the speed limit. Cleaned up after his dog. "What do I do, Carla, turn myself in?"

I laughed. "That doesn't seem necessary, Del."

"Well, then, I'll give something back." Del's eyes caught fire. "I'll build a chapel." He stretched his arm toward the back of his house. "A reading room for the community. With a lighted path. Open twenty-four hours for reading and sanc-tuary." I did a little dance. Del could reproduce Chartres for all I cared. I got to keep my tree.

I was lying in my place on a humid afternoon. I'd fallen in and out of sleep listening to the leaves, rocked, floating on the bay. Through the stone tracery around the Bradleys' side door, I could see the rubber-gloved hands of Marguerite at the sink, washing a cup, hanging it on the rack, washing a pot, drying it with a towel. Then, for a long time, she stood with her fin-gers spread under the steaming water, the rubber protecting her from the heat. I wondered if she enjoyed the feeling. When I awoke fully I saw that I wasn't eye level with my bed-room anymore. The branch was sagging under my weight. I shimmied down so that I was a few feet off the ground and let myself drop. A clump of brown leaves and bark spiraled down after me.

Over the next few days the leaves turned black and up-ward and fell like late November. I checked the notebooks at our town hall back to 1912 and found no record of oak wilt in this area. Gypsy moth can defoliate in two weeks, but I would have seen the caterpillars in early June. No canker-worms or oak worms. No gall. I checked depressions in the bark for oak scale. I should have been able to crack the case without staying up and seeing Del Bradley tiptoe between our houses with a five-gallon gas can of Velpar. Herbicide. Poi-son. I was born near a Christmas tree farm where Velpar was used to kill hardwoods. Del had poured on enough Velpar to defoliate the Everglades.

` ` `

The most important thing was to keep the tree cool and moist. I bought cork and tubes and some five-gallon bottles and made IVs. After midnight, when the porch lights had been turned off and the nervous flickering from televisions went black, I got to work. I drilled quarter-size holes in the bark and dripped water. I poured potassium chloride over the roots to knock the poison off the cell walls. Night after night I continued with the regimen, adding sugar to the water when the tree started running out of starch reserves, and soon it perked up, the leaves turned down, and the trunk stopped shedding. But I was no match for the Velpar. Again the branches drooped, and the bark became covered with stringlike threads. Through the night Del and I worked in shifts: I'd hydrate and feed; he'd pour on more Velpar. Finally, the only action worth taking was to remove the poison.

Through the night I shoveled, slamming the shovel into the dirt like I was staking a claim, stamping down on the blade with my foot, bending into the ground, my back screwing apart like a jar opening, dragging the bad dirt in lawn bags to a hole I'd made in the woods and scooping in new dirt around the roots. At times, this would occur to me: I wasn't just digging out the poison, I was *digging into* the tree. Deeper, higher, wider. I knew the complexity of its root system. I knew the insect and animal life that had lived and died beneath its body. I made a crawl space and backed down into the dirt. With my foot, I searched for cold places to warm with my body heat. I looked up through the roots and watched a fingernail moon cross the sky. For weeks there was dirt in my nails and scalp that wouldn't scrub out. The poison gave me a purple rash on my hands and face, as though I'd been slapped a thousand times.

The discomfort in my lower back had become intense. A tincture I prepared of lactuca leaf failed to bring relief, and the digging became torture. I'd also been having a considerable amount of lower abdominal pain and palpitation that I first attributed to stagnant blood or perhaps even a uterine fibroid. I tried tea and twice-weekly sitz baths of yarrow, but the pain worsened. Just to get to the bathroom I had to bend forward, tuck my head, and bring up my knees in a clumsy march. Del came to my door during this difficulty and asked me to step out to meet someone.

"This is Mr. Bohrman, Carla. Mr. Bohrman is a tree physiologist." I tilted up my head at this "tree physiologist," in his stiff plaid short sleeves and Naugahyde briefcase. He handed me his card from Wooded Acres Tree Service. "Mr. Bohrman has taken a look at the oak, Carla, and the prognosis is . . . Mr. Bohrman?"

His voice was soft. "Oak wilt is serious, ma'am."

"There's no oak wilt. Hasn't been oak wilt in this town in a century."

"Infected trees, like this one, ma'am, need to be destroyed. To save the others."

"Infected? You mean poisoned."

"Don't know what you mean," Del said.

"Ask him." I pointed at Del. "Ask him about the herbicide. Ask him. . . ." My knees buckled as the pain down below became unbearable.

Del caught me under the arms. My ovaries felt like they

were being ripped out by pliers. I slapped my feet against the stonework. "It's okay, Carla. I got you. Marguerite!" He yelled for his wife to call 911. I spit up yarrow tea down the front of my robe. Del got on his knees and smoothed back my hair. I was crying. "You just hold on to me, Carla." He took out a handkerchief and wiped my mouth. The tree physiologist bent down and offered his own handkerchief. And then, instantaneously, the pain stopped, flew out of me, and I felt light as powder. The euphoria of being free of pain made me laugh. Del laughed too. The tree physiologist stepped back and looked around nervously. Del gave me his hands and helped me stand. I was woozy but fine. Once I got my footing, I felt something inside me, heading down, slipping out. I watched it drop from under my robe and bounce on the stonework. A blood and mucus-streaked acorn, a perfect little oval in a cuplike hat—oh, a good inch and a half in diameter— wobbled down the incline and stopped dead between the tree physiologist's feet.

The next ones weren't nearly as strenuous in their passing. I'm not saying I *loved* passing acorns; I was dropping all over the house, and I'd wake each morning with a panty-load of fruit. But, like anything, it became part of the daily routine. I gathered them in baskets and vases and placed them next to family pictures on the mantel. As for Del and me, we got into an all-out offensive. He'd pour on the herbicide at two, I'd shovel and change dirt until dawn.

The sores and blisters on my hands from shoveling had opened to pink infant skin, blistered again, and opened, never enough time for scabbing. My ankles were swollen from edema; I had to leave my shoes unlaced to fit over my feet. I had something in my neck akin to whiplash. Heating pads and hydrastis brought little relief, until one morning I was too crippled to get out of bed. During the night I heard Del, his feet crunching the dead leaves, the soles of his boots padding the new dirt I'd laid. Get up, my mind said. Enough, my body replied.

I stayed in bed for three days, only struggling up for water or to use the bathroom. I'd stopped making acorns, with the exception of an occasional passing of something minuscule and misshapen. I bled.

On the third night a limb fell against the roof and woke me. I went to the window. Light from the street made shadows in the branches: a cat, a chair, a terrier on a leash. There was my father. Now he wore a hat with a brim. His shoes were polished. *You're on your own now.* He turned away from me, stepped up the branches into the crown, and disappeared in the leaves.

Later, the plastic on the window flung open and a storm blew into my room. A stream of leaves hovered over my bed. I rose to my knees. Leaves and bark slapped my face, pressed into my mouth to choke me, stuck in my hair, poked my eyes, until the wind lost momentum and the pieces of the tree piled on the floor.

In the morning I got up, showered, and dressed. I tidied up and had breakfast, a soft-boiled egg and mullein tea. Then I sat outside by the oak, some brown trumpet creeper straggling to my feet.

A group of laborers jumped off the back of a truck and

made their way across the lawn. Speaking in a foreign tongue I didn't know, they laughed and talked lightheartedly. They carried ropes and pushed a machine called a "stump remover," a yellow ice-cream cart over a whirling blade. The ropes were thrown into the low branches and cables were tightened, power lines were secured, and the hedge between Del's and my property was tied back. Then the foreman gave a signal and the door to the truck opened. From the cab, he slid down and limped and dragged himself across my yard: the cutter.

I stood and watched, my mind unable to process such a repugnant sight. Where there was supposed to be an arm there was a blade with continuous teeth and a motor. Where there was supposed to be a leg there were spikes on a metal thigh, blades on a steel calf. A clamp-on took the place of a foot. His hair was white, though he wasn't old, and woven into a braid that hung down to the top of his belt. His shirt was open despite the cold day, and I could see he had only one nipple. He came to me first. He knew me. He knew the whole story. A mocking grin spread over his face. He opened his lips. Where there were supposed to be teeth there were black holes between a scattering of gray stumps. Somehow I found my voice.

"You know . . . a tinture of oak bark packed around the gums can help that . . . particular kind of . . . dental problem."

He closed his mouth and stared into my eyes. Then he threw back his head and laughed, and all the men around him laughed too. But the sound of their laughter was soon swallowed by a horrible grinding, bone-crushing noise as the cutter reached under his metal arm and jerked a cord. The teeth on the chain blurred. He went up the trunk.

In seconds he was in the crown, black against the gray sky. I saw him shackle a branch in a rope and secure a cable. Then he swung the live saw around and held it to the wood. The branch plummeted, almost to the ground, but was wrenched up by the cables and held, twirling. The men scurried to the limb, unleashed it, threw it on a two-wheeled cart, and drew it to the street, where they hacked it into bits, inserted the smaller pieces into a chipper, and something resembling baby oatmeal sprayed out a bell-shaped chute. The bigger chunks were split and stacked on Del's woodpile.

He swung from branch to branch. As he cut, the sky came through, an endless gray vastness. Soon, there was just the stripped trunk and my branch, one arm praying.

I went inside. In my bedroom, I fell back on the floor against the wall, pulled my knees into my chest, crammed my thumbs into my ears. But the sound came through, a voice hoarse from screaming. Just for me, he left the last inch of branch to split, crack, and break on its own. Then there was a shaking of the house, with each block dropped from the trunk.

When I opened my eyes the cutter was before me, in my bedroom. I felt the heat from the saw, smelled the poison on his skin. My clothes dampened from the proximity of his sweat. He brought his face within inches of mine and spread his lips. Then he wedged his fingers into his mouth and squeezed what few teeth he had together. They slid across his gums until they were perfectly spaced. From the neck up, he looked almost normal now. He stood and stretched his neck and arm. Then he dragged himself across my room, tearing a gash in my rug, scratching the floor, and clinked and clanged down the stairs to the outside.

I was embarrassed, standing by Del's woodpile, seeing the tree this way, shape-shifted into something grotesque. I touched one of the logs. The bark was dry, powdery, and came apart in my hand. But beneath the outer skin and the sapwood, the older wood at the center was still hard and dense. They'd cut it alive. If I'd dug deeper; if my ridiculous body hadn't given out, a little rain, some sun; if only. . . . I spread my hand over a cross section. Then I heard Del behind me.

"Just so there are no bad feelings, Carla, I'd like to split the wood with you. There's a good four cord from all the cutting. I'll have my men stack it and cover it, and you're set."

I tasted blood. I wanted to bite out the inside of my mouth and swallow. I wanted to rise to twice my height and stretch into the shape of a crocodile jaw, my guts the teeth that would chew him up, my heart the tongue that would spit him among the trees, do to him what he'd done to me. But it was over. The jaw drew back into myself. I have to live here.

"Kind of you, Del. But there's trouble with my flue. Don't know that I'll be having fires this winter."

"I'll get over for a look-see in the morning."

"Don't want to put you out."

"No trouble."

I hadn't realized how much space it took. I never realized how big this house is, too big for one, but it is my home. For a while, I carried my acorns with me on long walks, planting them here and there. I flung fistfuls along the highway, tossed them on lawns and behind stores. I planted them down every median strip in town. Every park and school. Any green spot in a parking lot. I walked to where the town ends and the farms begin and planted in fields amid the barley and timothy. I found the tree farm near the place I was born and scattered them among the pines.

Christmas in my town: We do it up. Everyone's kids are home from school and the lawns are decorated with lights and ornaments. Heavy gray smoke floats up from the chimneys, the smell of wood and clove everywhere. In the morning I take a walk. Del steps out to wish me well, to invite me in for mulled wine, to talk about more building.

"We're putting in a pool, Carla. Indoor. Hope the noise won't be a bother."

" 'Course not, Del."

"I figure if I can't get Marguerite out . . ."

"Bring the outside in."

"Swimming would help that wrenching in your back. Open twenty-four hours for you."

"That's too generous."

"You're family."

Smoke curls over the lips of the chimneys, rolls down, curves around the trees and houses, circles my ankles, and rises up my legs. My skirt spreads into an umbrella. Smoldering holes open on my coat.

"You're on fire, Carla! Drop and roll!" Del shuffles sideways in front of me like he's trying to block a lineman. I turn and run.

"Now that's the worst thing to do. You're only feeding it. Marguerite!"

Fingers of flame run through my hair. My face foams into a blister. I lift off the ground into a cloud of smoke. Del jumps, trying to grab at my ankles. I shoot up like an arrow. I hover over Del's human-level trees, a row of hollies. I prick a finger on a spire atop Del's house and then fly off with the wind. Del's a speck. The houses are toys. Below me there are forests a thousand years old. And then color goes to white as my body shatters and seeds the clouds.

Painting House

On the night eighth grade let out, I was arrested for breaking into a storage shack behind a liquor store, looking for beer. I was fined $300, plus damages. My stepfather grounded me for the entire summer and said I had to work off the fine and damages by painting the entire inside of his enormous house. I told him painting was a boy's job. He told me that girls didn't get arrested, break into liquor stores, or smoke marijuana either. So I painted with my stepbrother, Phil, who was sixteen, and did whatever he told me to do. No room was ever finished. The painting went on and on. This room needed the windows scraped, that room needed another coat on the woodwork, and there was always another room that had to be scraped, sanded, spackled, taped, and painted.

ˋ ˋ ˋ

In July, my stepfather took my mother to South America. Phil
was left in charge.

Mom and I sat in the back of my stepfather's Jaguar and
looked out opposite windows on the way to the airport. She
wouldn't look at me. She once said she couldn't bear the way
I looked at her, as if everything were her fault and that I'd
been giving her that look since I was three. The fact was, I
didn't blame her for the state of things. If I harbored any
blame, it was for my stepfather, who'd appointed himself to
my personal discipline committee—a committee of one. I
once heard Mom tell Phil that she couldn't understand what
good could come out of all the grounding, but she wasn't going to go up against my stepfather. Mom didn't want to go to
South America. She hated uncomfortable travel because it reminded her of being poor, but my stepfather insisted. He
wanted to see Machu Picchu and Angel Falls. She wanted to
save her third marriage.

As we got closer to the airport, my mother started to worry
about missing the boat to the Galapagos.

"Ed and Foxy Miller took that boat and had to wait in
Guayaquil for six days," she said. "Ed says Guayaquil is the
armpit of the world."

My stepfather said that that was what travel was all about.
Travel was missing boats and getting stuck in terrible places,
and if they got stuck in Guayaquil for six *months,* then that's
what traveling was about.

My mother started to twist her gold necklace around her
finger. "Not to mention what Ed said about that boat. He said

that boat was the most uncomfortable experience of his life. Filthy. Sludge an inch thick everywhere."

My stepfather's silence said that this was also what travel was about. Travel was about sludge and filth and being uncomfortable, and if they died of malaria, if their tongues rotted out, and if their skin fell off inch by inch, then that was what travel was about. Then he yelled at Phil about haranguing him all the time for money. About how he'd never get into college with such piss-poor grades. About his driving. "The reason I never let you use the damn car in the first place is because you don't take care of anything. You're from the throwaway generation. Broken? Get a new one. Ask the druggie in the backseat how *hip* I am to your generation." Phil flipped on the blinker and moved into the right lane, careful to check over his shoulder and in the mirrors for other cars.

By the time we drove up the ramp to the airport, my mother's boat-travel stories had grown progressively worse, until three-quarters of the people on that boat had caught cholera and were floating for four days, not knowing where they were going. Phil stopped at the terminal entrance. "No monkey business in this car," my stepfather said, getting out. "I should have my head examined for letting you anywhere near it." My mother put her arms around me. I could hear her heart beating and could feel my own pulse in my head and an odd combination of familiar and unfamiliar sensations. Familiar, because this was my pretty mother with her large breasts and lily smell. Unfamiliar because she had stopped holding me when I was twelve. Now she was holding me hard.

"Why don't you climb up here?" Phil said, driving back. "So I don't feel like a chauffeur."

"No."

We drove in quiet and I looked out the window at all the things my mother had seen out her window on the way to the airport.

When we got home I told Phil I was going out. I said I'd made plans with my friend Amanda and Mom and Dad knew about it.

"I didn't know about it," Phil said.

I said I was going anyway and left. I didn't have plans. Amanda hadn't been my friend for two years. I walked up to McDonald's and sat outside. I bummed cigarettes from some of the tenth-grade girls and split a joint in the parking lot with Andy Spector, one of the boys I got arrested with for breaking into the storage shack.

"Your stepdad's a dick," Andy said. Andy's father had paid his fine and damages and said we were just acting the way kids act in the summertime. My stepfather said Andy's father was an alcoholic and what else could you expect.

I hung around outside McDonald's until they closed, and then walked home. Phil left the door unlocked so that I wouldn't have to dig the spare key out of the mulch around the dogwood. Going upstairs, I tried to keep quiet. I knew which creaky steps to avoid, even in the dark. Step over one to two, three, four, skip five, skip eight, stay by the wall on the landing, skip eleven.

Phil had moved into our parents' bedroom for the king-size bed and the TV.

"Karen," he called.

I pretended not to hear and went into my room and locked the door. I lay down on my bed with my clothes on, my eyes open in the dark.

"Karen," Phil whispered, and scratched the door with his fingernails. I don't know why he was whispering. Only the two of us were in the house.

The summer I was twelve, Phil came home from boarding school with a low voice and chest hair sticking out from the top of his T-shirt. I'd started my period while he was gone, and wearing a bra. Phil, who'd ignored me since my mother married his father five years before, looked me up and down, and I looked at him as if we were new people. Then he smiled and said I'd better watch out. One Saturday afternoon we were sitting on the floor of the rec room eating Cool Pops and watching a *Combat* rerun, and he started stroking my breasts through my shirt and my crotch through my shorts. I didn't stop him. I wanted someone to put his hands on me because I thought it would feel better than when I did it myself. We went on that way for the rest of the summer, and sometime during August, Phil said he wanted to take what we were doing to the next level. By this time he was moving my shirt away from my breasts and holding them in his hands, and he was wrapping his legs tightly around my thigh and rubbing himself against it. I knew "the next level" meant I'd have to touch him or even let him screw me, so I stopped everything. But he'd brush by me in the family room and I'd notice he smelled like Ivory Snow. Or we'd come face-to-face in the upstairs hall, move side to side trying to get by each other, and finally he'd move around me, leaving his soapy smell in every room he walked through.

The following spring he came home from school with a rough face and a stocky build from wrestling and lifting weights. He'd learned things: how to give a girl an orgasm with his fingers, and that if you use your tongue on a girl she'll do anything. I wouldn't do *anything,* but I liked his tongue, so I let him screw me. And then we were doing it wherever we could, whenever our parents went out. Phil wanted to do it while my mother was home, when she was out back weeding, or meeting with her investment club, or when our parents had the Millers over for drinks, to just quickly, quietly, let him stick it in, but I wouldn't let him while they were there. And I still wouldn't touch him. He wanted me to do it with my hand and he wanted me to put my mouth on it. I couldn't even bear to guide it in and I never looked at it. Every time we did it I swore it would be the last time, and he'd say that was just fine and tiptoe back down the hall to his room.

Nonetheless, it continued. We worked out bargains. There were conditions and rules that were understood and honored. Miraculously, I didn't get pregnant. In fact, it never occurred to me until he brought it up that I could get pregnant. I assumed the secretiveness and the danger were themselves sufficiently prophylactic. And soon he started talking about taking what we were doing to an even higher level.

But now I wanted it to stop. I felt with our parents gone I could stop it. Their absence empowered me; I was the woman of the house. We weren't the children anymore and I had a say. Phil saw things differently. We had a house. A king-size bed. We could do it all night like a real couple.

In the morning I told Phil I didn't want to do it with him anymore. That was all I said. He was reading the box scores in *The Post* and didn't look up. I said I really meant it this time. He wrinkled his forehead, brought his hands together to turn the page, and still didn't look at me. I took my cereal bowl to the sink and heard him say, just above a whisper, *"Do* what? You don't *do* anything." I pretended not to hear and washed the morning dishes and the plate and glass from Phil's snack the night before.

After breakfast we went to the paint store for more cans of linen white. Phil always insisted we get to the store when it opened so that we could watch the professional painters pick up their supplies.

The painters were men who looked older than they were. They were either rail thin, or oddly fat with muscular arms and huge guts. At seven o'clock in the morning they reeked of tobacco and their fingers were stained yellow. Some of them had shaky hands as they reached for new rollers or pointed out the paints they wanted mixed. Phil knew about some of them.

"See that one? He has a master's degree in anthropology. He says he's a painter because he just likes to paint," Phil whispered, and shook his head sympathetically. "See that one? He was quarterback for Central. He used to be a good-looking guy. Then he was living on the street, draining the alcohol out of Sterno." They all had a story. They all fell from something great to being painters. I felt we were playing with something dangerous by being there, that if we got too close to these men, whatever had grown inside them that made them amount to nothing but painters would come off on us. Phil and I were merely passing through, painting for the summer. These guys were stuck.

"Ahhh," Phil sighed, kneeling on the living room floor, inhaling the fumes off the top of a freshly pried-open can of paint. He loved the smells: the mineral scent of oil base, the sharp pine bouquet of paint thinner and turpentine. Even a new brush has a distinctly sweet chemical odor.

"Straight up, straight down, Karen," Phil suggested rather than ordered. He never barked orders, and when I did something well he praised me, made it seem as if it were my idea in the first place. "Try smaller strokes, that's right. Loosen up your wrist or you'll get tired. Relax. You're being too hard on yourself. That's it. Beautiful job. You want to rest? Go ahead." I'd sit against a dry wall and smoke and watch him painstakingly sand the woodwork with the finest-grain sandpaper. "Sand after each coat so it's smooth," he said. "And always paint with the grain. When that dries we'll sand again and put on another coat." I hated sanding so Phil never made me do it. But I loved painting after he'd sanded, like putting frosting on a warm cake.

I was putting a third coat on some molding when I felt hands on my sides and the sensation of an electric sting shoot down my spine. Phil grabbed me around the waist, put his foot between mine and tripped me, bringing me to the floor. "Takedown," he said. He slipped one arm around the back of my thigh and cradled my neck with the other. "Pinning combination." I stayed still, waiting for it to be over. Soon he took his arm away from my thigh and put his hand between my legs. I pushed it away. He propped himself up on his elbows. "We're taking the rest of the day off." He was still breathing hard from the wrestling move. "We're going on a picnic."

We made sandwiches and packed some fruit and stopped at the grocery for drinks. I had some pot and we sat on a bench in the park and laughed at people, tried to remember the theme music from *McHale's Navy,* and kept getting it mixed up with *Hogan's Heroes.* But then Phil started to come down from the pot and got in one of his bad moods. Why did I wear shorts? he wanted to know. Why didn't I wear a dress so that he could screw me in the woods, and why wouldn't I kiss him?

"I don't own a dress," I said.

"I want you to kiss me," he said. He'd been trying to kiss me all summer but I wouldn't kiss him. Girlfriends kissed their boyfriends, and we weren't boyfriend and girlfriend. "It's not normal," Phil said. "Not to kiss somebody. You kiss me or everything stops."

"Everything *has* stopped," I said.

He put his face in his hands, and I saw his back shaking up and down because he was crying. I hadn't seen him cry since he'd gotten beaten up in the seventh grade by eighth-graders for being a pip-squeak and he looked just as weak and pathetic now as he did then.

That night he asked where I was going. "None of your goddamn business," I said, and walked to McDonald's. Phil stayed two blocks behind me the whole way. I stood in line for an orange drink, and Phil came in and stood next to me. He told me to get something more, he'd pay. I walked over to a booth where some of the tenth-grade girls were smoking cigarettes and drinking Diet Cokes. I asked them for a cigarette. They let me sit with them while I smoked it. One of the girls was Kim Roston. Kim was the most popular girl in my junior high school when I was in eighth grade and she was in ninth. All the boys wanted her but she went for bigger stock. Her boyfriends were in high school, and now that she was going into high school, she wanted to meet boys in college. She held her cigarette between two French-manicured nails, took a slow drag, blew a smoke ring, then let the rest waft upward. Her best friend, Sharon Day, kept an eye on the parking lot, looking for someone who'd give them a ride to a concert at the college.

I saw Phil over by the doors step in front of a girl he knew, hands in his pockets, with a cigarette dangling from his lip like a gangster in a movie. He looked down at her, stood too close, and moved from side to side so that she couldn't get around him. Finally he let her go, and she moved away blushing.

"Karen," Kim Roston said. I didn't know she knew my name. "Your stepbrother's cute." I had never noticed until Kim pointed it out that he really was cute. He wasn't tall. By the time I was thirteen we were eye to eye, but he was broad and strong. He had a thick, powerful neck, round copper eyes, and long, black, straight hair.

Sharon spotted a boy she knew circling the parking lot in a tan Dodge. It wasn't ideal, but it was a ride. The girls gathered cigarettes and bags, jangled charm bracelets, and checked for lipstick on their teeth in compact mirrors. I thought they might ask me along but they smiled politely and said good-bye. Then the only people in McDonald's were Phil and me. He was sitting at a table by the doors. We looked at each other and looked away. He pretended not to notice me walking out. He'd gotten busy with the hem of his jeans as though there were something wrong with it. When I passed his table he looked out the window to the far end of the parking lot as if there were someone out there he knew.

The hill leading down to the tracks behind McDonald's had fresh mud from that morning's rain. I held my arms out like a surfer and slid down. I looked back and saw Phil standing at the top of the trail. He surfed down after me. I started walking down the tracks. "We live the other way," he called. He followed behind me and I picked up my pace. I walked as fast as I could, swinging my arms to go faster. Phil jogged behind me. I started to run. He kept up. Soon my breath got short and I had to stop. "Can we please turn around now?" he said.

"You can," I said.

"I'm responsible for you. I promised Mom and Dad." I kept walking, picking up speed as I got my breath back. "Oh, fuck it," he said finally, and walked in the other direction. I stopped and watched him. Five yards down he stopped and looked all around himself. "Look," he said. The entire ravine was lit in green by fireflies, millions of them, glowing in the trees and bushes and hovering overhead. I walked back to where Phil was standing and we watched together. He captured a bug in his hands and opened them slightly so that I could see it light up the small hollow space. "If you squeeze the stuff out of them it'll keep glowing on your hand for a minute."

"Let's do it," I said. He shook his head. "I want to see."

"I don't want to kill it," he said. He gave me the bug so that I could watch my own hands light up.

"I want to try it," I said. Phil walked on without me. I let the bug go.

As we followed the tracks homeward, Phil picked up some gravel and asked me how much I wanted to bet he could hit that tree with a rock, or that beer can, and we tried to see who could walk on the rail the longest without falling off. I got ten feet before I slipped but Phil stayed on, even jumped over to the other rail without falling. Soon he got bored with walking on the rail and came down to the ties, and I got up on the rail and held on to his shoulder for balance until I got bored. Then we walked on the ties, which were placed too close together for walking, mismatched with the human stride, so we stepped in between or hopscotched them, two or three at a time.

I went to the library to see if a book could explain why I was so swollen and itching between my legs. I was certain I'd contracted a disfiguring venereal disease but found I just had a case of vaginitis. The book was old and prescribed a cornstarch bath as a remedy. Phil came into the bathroom while I was in the tub and looked at my nipples, which stuck out of the cornstarch water like berries in milk. I slid down so that he couldn't see anything.

"It's okay. I'm not going to do anything," he said. "I came in to tell you we're going out to dinner." I hadn't been out anywhere except McDonald's all summer. "And there's a present. An apology present. For everything." He stood at the door looking at me and I slid down further, until the water was up to my eyes.

My present was carefully laid across my bed. It was a dress. It was thin, soft cotton with a tiny rose pattern on a purple background, with a zipper below a round opening in the back. It fit tightly at my waist and flared slightly at my hips. The neckline was a simple scoop and the sleeves were capped. Except for smudges of linen white that wouldn't wash off my elbow, the back of my knuckles and the tops of my shins, I thought I looked like a model.

We drove to The Magic Pan in the Jaguar. Phil said he liked the Jag fine but if you wanted to mess with a British car you'd better have a degree in electrical engineering. But all I could think of was how the rose material of the dress looked against my sand-colored knees and where the sleeves stopped and the freckled skin of my arms began. At the restaurant I ordered a piña colada and the waitress brought it to me, never questioning my age. I crossed my legs. I lit a long Eve ciga-rette and smoked. After dinner we went for a walk around the playground at the park. I swung on the candy-cane-painted swing set and Phil threw pebbles though a basketball hoop. I opened my legs and let the air blow through the skirt of my dress while I swung.

We walked across a bridge over the creek to a field of base-ball diamonds, and Phil talked about cars and wrestling and college and how he was thinking of not going right away, maybe joining the merchant marine or traveling for a year. I felt the dress grazing the back of my thighs, the material clinging to my waist. He put his hand on my back, where the dress was open, and I reached around and pushed it away. But soon his hand sneaked back and I let him keep it there.

When we got home I went to my room and locked the door and took off my shoes and underwear. I lay on my stomach and reached back and unzipped my dress, pretending it was my husband's hand unzipping it for me, and my husband's hands taking it off. After I took off my dress I lay naked with my imaginary husband. We weren't going to have sex, we were just going to be naked together, the way people who have been married a long time can just be naked together and think nothing of it.

My mother called from Guayaquil. I ran downstairs to take the call. My stepfather had gone on to the Galapagos but she'd stayed in Guayaquil because she wouldn't go on that boat. She wanted to come home but was afraid to fly alone, so she was waiting at the hotel for my stepfather, and Ed Miller was right, Guayaquil was the worst place in the world. Then she said she needed to get back so that she and I could get settled in St. Petersburg, Florida, before the school year started. St. Petersburg because her mother lived there and my mother said I could use a grandparent. I asked her where we'd live: Would we live in a house or would we have to live in an apartment?

"I don't know," she said.

My stepfather had a lot of money, I said. So we'd get a lot of money, right?

"I just don't know."

I told my mother that at least I wouldn't be grounded anymore, and was serious, but she laughed her sweet laugh, which I hadn't heard in a long time. The sound hit me some-where between my stomach and hips like a tickle, and I felt myself go limp. I stumbled and sat on the floor. I said more things I knew would make her laugh. Then I told her I wanted a horse. She said, "We'll see."

When there was nothing left to say the call got discon-nected, as though only the sound of her voice could keep the line alive. I stood at the window. Outside, my stepfather's im-peccable lawn swept down to the street. A man jogged by with a collie. The headlights from a station wagon tore a swatch in the darkness. I walked from room to room. The street lamps shone through the windows, lighting up ghosts: the sheet over the dining room table like an elegant cloth, ready to be set for dinner; the drop cloth over the piano sway-ing slightly; a phantom audience of chairs. There was so much more painting to be done but I didn't feel overwhelmed by it anymore because I'd already moved to Florida. I was already living in a big house with a pool and picking oranges in our yard and playing with my horse. I gathered some paint stirrers that were spread around the mantel and on the floor and piled them on top of a paint can. I checked that the front door was locked. I closed a window in the living room be-cause it had started to rain, and picked up the freshly washed towels on the stairs.

Phil lay on his father's side of the bed reading *Sports Illus-trated*. When he saw me leaning against the door of our par-ents' bedroom, he put down the magazine and stared. It was the first time I'd ever let him look at me naked, all at once, not parts at a time. I stood there for a long time because now

I wanted him to see me. He held the covers open and I got in the huge bed with him. He rolled onto his side and propped himself up on one elbow so he could look. He said I was pretty red between my legs and asked if it was very uncomfortable. I said I was feeling a lot better, especially since I'd found out I didn't have gonorrhea, and he laughed. He wanted to kiss me and I let him. And then we were like a couple, like a married couple in a king-size bed. For the next five days, while we waited for my mother, we painted together, we took walks after dinner, we held hands, we kissed good night.

He Came Apart

His hair comes out in my hands. Two clumps of golden straw. The bare spots on his head like those mysterious circles carved in Scottish wheat fields. I reach back in and pull gently. "No more." He jolts up in bed. "Stop messing with me. For God's sake, leave it alone!" Ridiculously, I try to put it back. I balance the little nest on top of his head and chase him to the mirror; he wants to see if it's really true. Later in the shower, the rest of it washes off his head and clogs the drain.

"No male-pattern baldness, anywhere in your family, ever? No change of diet? No medications? No harsh detergents?"

"No. No. And no. You're humiliating me. Stop."

I go through the checklist again and we start quarreling.

He's furious with me for being insensitive, for thinking only of myself because I begin a phase-one environmental investigation of our flat, where we meet every Tuesday, Thursday, and Friday afternoons and some evenings if we can get away, trying to find poison, discoloration in the water, dusty air vents, anything, wondering what it would do to my career if I lost *my* hair. I stop short in the kitchen, thinking of my husband's thick silver hair, which grayed in his early twenties, and how beautiful it is. I want to go home, but I can't leave Gus this way.

I come up behind him as he stands before the bathroom mirror, looking back and forth between his sudden baldness and his eyebrows, which have rubbed off in his hands. "Bald men are sexy," I try to reassure. "And who needs eyebrows?" I think about what I'd do if I lost mine. I could pencil them in, but that always looks fake. He stomps back to the bedroom, flops down on the chaise, and clicks the remote. CNN has footage of the plane crash off Greenland. There were two babies on board. People had actually put on life vests, believing there was such a thing as a water landing. I need to see my son. "Gus, sweetheart, I know it's bad timing, but I have to leave. I have to do my special twenty minutes with William."

"Fine. Go. I have no claim here." He clicks the remote to C-SPAN and, just like that, his thumb flies off his hand. We look at each other in horror for a moment, then fall to our knees in a frenzied search. "Surgeons have revolutionized this type of reconstruction," I say with my head under the chaise. But by the time I discover the thumb under the ottoman, it has shriveled to the size of a peanut shell and a thick film of bluish skin has grown over the wound on Gus's hand.

"Don't be pouty," I say, buckling the belt on my dress. "Your hair will grow back. I love you still."

"Go do your special twenty minutes." He's looking in our empty refrigerator.

"Put your arms around me." He turns to face me and as he wraps me in his arms, the right one tumbles to the floor.

Amid the chaos, the alarms, and shouting, my own face mocks me from the magazine rack by the checkout counter. Soda cans explode in the aisle like grenades, an elderly woman has slipped on some banana pudding, grapefruits bounce from their display, and balloons saying CRAZY AU-TUMN SAVINGS try to escape through the ceiling. Security guards rush by, their heavy soles clomping on the linoleum, their keys and cuffs tinkling. And there I am. Three covers in one month. *Mothers Day, Parents This Week,* and the palace coup *Pretty Mom.* I stare back at myself as the store falls in around me. This is my problem, I know, my son, but like the manager taking the ball from a spent pitcher, the store personnel are going to have to take over. "Here's the little whippersnapper." A guard hands me my four-year-old, forcing him into the seat of the cart and strapping him down with the seat belt. I fit a bag of Skittles into his hand. "And may I just say you are even more beautiful in person than you are on the *Phlufff* . . . box?" I smile and thank the guard, though I'm horribly embarrassed about all the trouble. Crystal, the checkout woman, reaches for the groceries on the conveyor belt.

"He senses your absence, Jeanette." She nods toward William as Cocoa Puffs, Bugles, Eggos, Hawaiian Punch,

Doritos, and Doughnut O's shuttle across the scanner. "He knows your heart is elsewhere. He acts out. End things with Gus. Cold turkey." As she says this, DELI reads out on the register screen. "You owe it to yourself. You owe it to Frank. You owe it to little Will." She hits the button, which tallies up the groceries for my family. Then comes the part I hate, when she scans the groceries for Gus and me. Vegetable pâté, gherkins, sparkling cider, herbal tea, kosher salt, natural beer, artichokes. She holds up a bag of something she doesn't recognize.

"Star fruit," I say. She frowns at the price, then puts on half-eye glasses and examines a vegetable that looks like a bed of baby snakes. "Fiddlehead ferns. I'm not ready to give him up, Crystal. Especially now. He's sick. He needs me."

"Hmpf." She hits the tally on the second set of groceries. The nine items are nearly as expensive as the cartful of food for my family. I push the OK button on the ATM and move out.

There's no answer when I try to call Gus from the Eau d'Oeuvre cologne shoot. I start to leave a message on Frank's voice mail when the director shouts from the set, "I need Mommy and the B.O.M. Let's go, people." B.O.M. is for baby-of-the-moment, which their mothers hate because they know they're out on the street in a matter of months, sometimes weeks. I stand in front of a huge orange seamless sheet of paper; I'm dressed in a yellow tennis skirt, a yellow polo, and yellow sneakers. The director snatches Averille from his mother. Averille is supposed to be a girl in the ad, so he's referred to by the crew as April. He's got a big yellow bow on his head and he's wearing a white ruffled dress. The pinkest cheeks I've ever seen, the sweetest smile. An angel. "All yours." I take him in my arms. He coos and snuggles into my chest. Sure enough, the smell of him makes my milk run. Because of all the shoots I've done with babies, I never stopped lactating after I weaned William. The way they smell, their soft skin, their downy hair, the way they seem to love you, I never have the chance to dry up.

We shoot the Happy Baby Segment, *the baby whose mommy wears Eau d'Oeuvre cologne.* I skip around the set swinging my hips so that the skirt will flounce. April nearly gets whiplash but doesn't mind a bit, which is why he gets so much work. Between takes he burrows into me, squeezes the material of my shirt, and rubs his leg against my belly. Milk spills out of my breasts, soaking my polo shirt. The crew is prepared. I strip to the waist right there on the set, dry off with a hand towel, and dress in an identical shirt and bra. Then a trampoline is dragged out; April and I climb on. I do a series of jumps against the orange backdrop, a c-jump, an a-jump, a stag. My breasts are killing me; I wish I'd worn a sports bra. But April loves it. His head jerks back and he laughs and screams for more. The director good-nights me, April's mother is sent off the set, and the crew sets up for the Sad Baby Segment, *the baby whose mommy doesn't wear Eau d'Oeuvre cologne.* The stage manager seats April on the trampoline and makeup brushes on powder to take the blush out of his cheeks. A child psychologist is brought out and situated to the right of the cameraman. The camera moves in tight on April.

"Rolling," the director says. "Action."

"No." The psychologist shakes a finger at the baby. "No, no, no, no." April sobs. It's a wrap.

Averille's mother has been waiting for me in the parking lot. She puts her hand on my arm.

"Jeanette, you've been through a lot of babies. Does Averille have a chance? Of going to the next level? Do you think he could be like Nevada Rhodes?" Nevada Rhodes was the baby I posed with on the *Phlufff* . . . box fifteen years ago. He went on to do features.

I hate this. "I'm going to tell you what I tell all the mothers. Save. Invest. There's only one Nevada Rhodes." I leave her biting her nails by the open door of the black BMW 700-series sedan that she bought with Averille's money.

I have a meeting in an hour at a school we're looking at for William, but Gus still isn't answering the phone so I race over to the flat.

"Why didn't you answer? I've been calling."

He's under a blanket on the chair-and-a-half in the living room, rocking himself from side to side.

"I'm afraid to move."

He pulls the cover back to show me he's had a leg off.

"My God. Did you call the doctor?"

"Hell no. Never call a doctor for anything serious. Besides, this has nothing to do with medicine. This is God casting his net."

"I think God has bigger problems, Gus, you know, like that avalanche in Switzerland and that flood in Texas." I drop a foot-filled Reebok in a lawn-and-leaf bag.

"I see you're as capable of deep feeling as ever."

"Let's not fight." I scan the room for the leg. "Come on, I'll help you." He puts his arm around my shoulder and hops next to me to the bedroom. I help him into bed and pull up the quilt.

"Lie down next to me?" His teeth are chattering. I feel his forehead for fever.

"I have a meeting. A new school for William." I tuck the quilt around him.

"Please? I'm terrified."

I pull back the quilt and slide in next to him. He holds me in his arm and puts his leg over my legs. He kisses me. I love the way he smells. I once tried to re-create it in the kitchen: cayenne and rosemary, sweat and leaves. He moves my blouse aside with his face. "I don't have time," I whisper. He gently bites a nipple through my shirt. I raise my chest. "Mmmm."

"Can I still come with you when you get them done?" Recently he'd teased me about getting my little breasts augmented.

"Sure."

"I'll pay." He nibbles the other one.

"Ohhhhhh. But I can afford them. I can afford to put breasts on the entire U.S. Olympics gymnastics team."

"Then I want to pay half."

"What about the debt?" I whisper in his ear.

"What debt?" He starts moving his hips against mine.

"What I'll owe you. Ten years from now, when we positively repulse each other, when you've dumped me for something younger. Do you still have rights?"

"Just to the left one." He unbuttons my blouse and pulls down my bra.

"So my husband gets the right one?" He stops moving and

turns away from me, stares up at the recessed lighting we had put in the ceiling. "What's wrong?"

"That's the part I can't stand. I know he's your husband, but does he have to have one of your breasts?"

"How can I reassure you?"

"With constancy." He kisses me and puts his remaining hand on my left breast. It's still there when he rolls away.

What a beautiful school, an old mansion converted. The kids on the playground look happy and clean. As I walk up the wooden steps I say a little prayer: "Please, accept us. Accept us, please."

I'm told to make myself at home in the director's office while we wait for her to come back from a tour. Frank arrived before me and has taken over her phone and desk. His brief-case is open on a couch and his mechanical pencils are strewn about the floor. He's carrying on two arguments, one with an investment banker on a cell phone and the other with the S.E.C. on the director's phone.

"I hope I'm not late," I whisper. He gestures for me to sit. "You look great," I say. I look at his hair, which is silver and thick and long. The veins on his hands and forearms are pulsating with strength.

"*Sonzafuckingbitches.*" He hangs up both phones. We stare at each other for a few moments.

"God, I miss you, Frank. I miss you so much I could die from it." Like a kid on Christmas trying to catch a glimpse of Santa, I stay awake as long as I can each night in hopes of seeing my husband, or at least try to wake as he's leaving. But he slips out with the other shadows of the morning before

I'm conscious. A tear spills out of my eye and rolls down my face.

"This stuff is so damn complicated, Jeannie. I'm barely hanging on."

"You're at the top of your game, Frank. By millions."

"Nah. I'm just on a streak."

"You've been on a streak for five years."

"These things can just disappear, Jeannie. I can be on the street in five minutes."

"What's so bad about the street?" The school director says good luck to another couple, then comes through the door, shakes our hands, tells me I'm prettier than the *Phlufff* . . . box, and proceeds to show us around the school.

"Trigonometry?" I ask, looking in a room of kindergartners who are deep in study.

"They can handle it, Jeanette. And, believe it or not, we make it fun!" She leads us up a creaky staircase to the higher classes, Frank's jacket sleeve brushing against the cool skin of my arm. "Don't you adore Proust?" A third-grade class is reading aloud from *Remembrance of Things Past,* but I'm conscious only of Frank's hand on the back of my waist, the citrus smell of his hair gel.

"Do you think we'll get in?" I ask Frank as we walk to our cars.

"Bill Krist's sister-in-law is the former director of admissions. That'll help. You've cultivated that relationship, right?"

I scan my mental date book. "Yes. We had lunch in January and I called when her father was ill."

"See you at home." He opens the back door of his car.

"Will you?"

"Jeannie . . ."

"I'm so lonely, Frank."

"Get a sitter. Go out. Have fun. Kiss kiss." His driver whisks him away as he presses the auto-dial on his cell phone.

Gus. I call our nanny Patrice from the car phone to ask her to pick up Will, then race over to the flat. As I pull into the gravel driveway I remember it was Esperanza's day to clean and I'm immediately relieved that Gus had company. The house is immaculate; Esperanza is an excellent cleaner. I don't hear a sound. I feel a pit in my stomach as I race through the house.

"Hello?" he calls finally from the bedroom.

"I was so worried. Are you all right?"

"Nothing new to report," he says. "Everything's intact." I breathe a sigh as I enter the bedroom. He's propped up on pillows. A drink with a straw sits on the bedside table. As I bend to kiss him I notice he smells like my honeysuckle soap. He's dressed in an orange-and-blue rugby shirt, orange shorts, and an orange sock. I like each of the elements alone—in fact, I bought them—but not all together.

"You look like a flag."

"Esperanza dressed me."

"She's a lifesaver." He seems cheerful, which is good because I have no time to spend. I have a screening tonight. I have to finish William's cow costume for Farm Day at his nursery school, write a recommendation for a neighbor's kid to get into Will's pre-school, and ask another neighbor to write a recommendation for Will to get into the Mardel school. And I still haven't done my twenty minutes of special time that the psychologist recommended I spend with William every day.

"I can't stay. What can I get you before I flee?"

He takes a long breath. "I need to tell you something. It's going to upset you, but I have to tell you because I have to be honest with you, because I've always been honest with you, because our relationship is based on honesty." I feel my insides drop to the base of my torso. It always begins with honesty.

"Who? Your old girlfriend?" He won't answer. "Tell me. It's Leslie, right?"

"No, it's not Leslie."

I look around the room, at how spotless everything is. "No, not Esperanza."

"I'm sorry, Jeanette."

I break down in tears.

"Oh, Jeanette. It would be a farce for us to say we'll be faithful to each other. That's a marriage. We're not married. *You're* married. To someone else. I have a problem in this direction, I told you when I met you. I love you. You're beautiful. Why would you be jealous?"

"I don't know, just an emotion that's dogged me my whole life."

I look down at him on the bed. He's all I have. My only oasis. A respite from all the madness. "I have to go."

"I love you."

"Try not to move." I blow my nose. "You stay intact when you don't move."

"When will I see you?"

"I'll come back tonight."

` ` `

There's a message on my voice mail from my agent saying I've been nominated for Pretty Mom of the Year. She's also got a commercial for Your Silver Year Nutrient Shake. "I know you're *nowhere near* fifty," she says apologetically. I dress for the screening and as I'm heading out the door I remember I haven't done my special twenty minutes with William. "I'll make it up to you," I whisper in his ear as he's watching *Gladiator Space Phenetians* on public TV. "I owe you two hours and forty minutes. Imagine what we can do with all that." He raises his shoulder to rub his ear as though a bug had crawled in. I ask Patrice to finish painting the spots on the cow costume.

The screening is a made-for-TV movie starring the baby I posed with on a hundred spots and magazine covers, the baby who smiles up at me on the *Phlufff . . .* box, who is now fifteen years old. As with so many events, I go alone. I stand by the ashtrays in the lobby and consider calling Gus from the pay phone but I'm still upset about Esperanza. Then I think about leaving a voice mail for Frank. People from the industry say hello and indiscreetly ask where Gus is. No one asks where my husband is anymore.

"I know you." It's the actor Austin Kairys. I feel myself blush. I've had a crush on him ever since he played Cyrus Vance in *Rescue '80.* I can't believe he's talking to me.

"You look so much younger in person." What a stupid thing to say.

"And you are more beautiful than the *Phlufff . . .* box."

"Oh, stop."

He takes a bag of popcorn from a tray carried by a pretty girl in a French maid costume. Never taking his eyes from me, he shakes a few kernels in his hand and tosses them back in his mouth. There's a hush in the crowd and flashbulbs pop as Nevada Rhodes walks in with his albino girlfriend. A gang of howling twelve-year-old girls are held back by security. The paparazzi have always loved our reunions. Mother and son. A spotlight on top of a TV camera makes me squint as Nevada kisses me on both cheeks. It never fails. The smell of Nevada makes my milk flow. Tonight I came prepared, wearing cotton pads in my dress. He whispers in my ear, "Jeanette, I'm getting married." The photographers are on top of us. I'm smiling for the cameras but what I really want to do is slap this spoiled boy.

"But you're so young. Don't do this." I want the baby Nevada back. When he was dressed like a girl. When he smelled like powder. When his hair was as wispy as cashmere.

"I'm in love." He kisses me on the mouth for the cameras. It's more than I can handle. My milk spills over, seeps right through the pads. Two huge circles appear on my silk dress. Nevada moves away, spotting the star of the *Fast Cats* series.

"Nevada, come back. Listen to me." I reach out for him but he sinks into the crowd, and photographers fill in the space behind him. Austin Kairys wraps his jacket around my shoulders.

I leave before the credits and head over to see Gus. He's had a bad night. In the foyer there's a large joint I assume is his knee. Some teeth are strewn around the phone. Did he try to call? There's an ear on an end table, and under the love seat, a skin bag that resembles a tobacco pouch. "I told you not to move," I cry. He's on the floor in the kitchen.

"I was hungry."

"I left a sandwich by the bed. And magazines. Everything you could need."

"The sandwich was so good, I wanted more."

I carry what's left of him to the bedroom and lay him down. As I'm fixing the pillows I glance over at the clock. It's midnight. Occasionally Frank surprises me and comes home this early. "I'm not going to be able to stay. But you've got to promise you won't move."

"How was the screening?" Gus rolls on his side and clicks the remote control with his chin. A Sky King crashed on the interstate. Six businessmen are killed. I need to get home. I close the blinds and pick his clothes up off the floor, shaking them first to make sure they're empty. "Nevada Rhodes, that little baby. That fifteen-year-old. He says he's getting married."

"To the albino? What the hell's wrong with everybody that they want to get married?"

"It will be terrible for him." I move Gus back onto the pillows. He purses his lips for me to kiss him; I pretend not to notice.

"All relationships are doomed," he says.

"What a thing to say." I pull the blanket over his chest.

"Imagine having the life sucked out of you at fifteen."

"Is that what I do to you?" I straighten up and put my hands on my hips. "Am I sucking the life out of you?" He doesn't answer. The news has footage of the screening:

Nevada Rhodes walking into the theater, kissing me, shaking hands with the star of *Fast Cats,* and in the upper right side of the screen, Austin Kairys wrapping his jacket around my shoulders. I look at Gus to see if he's noticed. He has.

"Uhhh huh. Austin Kairys. Mr. Secretary."

"I had an accident through my dress. He came to the rescue."

"Give you his pants too?"

"Don't be preposterous. I have to go. Kiss kiss. Don't move." It's after one when I get home. I put on perfume and a French lace slip and try to stay awake long enough to see Frank. I fail.

I put a quarter in the slot of the mechanical rocking horse. It gets jammed. The arcade manager tells me I must have put something other than a quarter in there because he's been running this place since the seventies and never had any trouble with the horse. I tell him no, it was definitely a quarter. He says fine, whatever you say, and offers to refund the quarter. I say that I don't care about the money, I just want my son to be happy. When, does he imagine, will the horse be fixed?

"Tuesday."

"Then we shall return on Tuesday."

"I'll leave the lights on." He wanders off into the hell of blinking ray guns and bells as I take William down from the lame horse.

The zoo got new polar bears. "Look how cute," I say. Last year some kids climbed over the bars and were eaten. The police opened up the bears to look for them. William asks me where the old bears went, though I know he knows. "To the North Pole to live with Santa." Over on the grass there's a family unpacking a picnic lunch on a blanket.

"I'm hungry," William says.

"You're hungry? Didn't Patrice give you lunch?" He doesn't answer; he looks over at the picnic. We line up at a cart for a hot dog. The woman on the grass is opening plastic containers. There's a rice salad, a carrot salad, a pasta salad, a green bean salad, and some fruit salad. And there's fresh bread wrapped in foil and a thermos of juice and something for dessert, which the woman says is a surprise. She gives the man and the boy on the blanket forks and cloth napkins. The man's having trouble getting the baby's socks on because the baby keeps moving. The lady says it's okay for the baby to go barefoot, they're on a blanket after all. The boy flips his fork and tries to catch it by the handle. The man holds the baby up in the air.

"I want salad," William says.

"I thought you liked hot dogs."

"I want salad." He starts to cry. We wander around the zoo for half an hour looking for salad. Then he says he wants to go home and have lunch again with Patrice.

In the car William stares out the back and won't talk. I guess we both thought the day would be different.

Star Gaze has photos from the Nevada/albino wedding. They eloped after the screening. I shouldn't have left early. Maybe I could have stopped them. "Your little baby. All grown up," Crystal says, flipping through the rag.

"Don't be cruel. Not today." Nevada looks so handsome in his Nehru tux. A tear drips off my face and onto the conveyor belt. Crystal and I watch as it moves across and gets pulled down into the mechanical world.

In the car, I check my voice mail for a message from Gus. How pathetic. We share a flat. His limbs have fallen off. He has no ears, no hair, only a scattering of teeth. His nose hangs by mucous beads. I *still* wait for him to call. There's a message from my agent: "Big news! Call me!" A message from Austin Kairys saying no rush getting back his jacket, but how 'bout returning it over lunch? I play it back a few times, just to make sure. And then Gus telling me he's sorry he didn't call earlier, he slept all day, no rush coming over. But I rush over anyway.

Gus is arranged on the bed like bones on an anthropological dig. "Who laid you out? Esperanza?"

"Ain't she a wonder." He's staring at an infomercial for an instant miracle teeth whitener. I bring him a Natural Beer with an extra-long straw that I bought at the toy store. "Oh, a letter came from your agent. By, uh, Fed Ex. You got Pretty Mom of the Year again."

"Fabulous."

"You don't seem happy."

I shrug.

"What are you going to do with the Plymouth?"

"Give it away."

"Why not keep it? Strap me in. Push me off a cliff."

"Stop." I rub his head. "I want you to come with me. To the awards ceremony."

"As what? Your seat cushion?"

"As my date. As the love of my life."

"Silver-headed Frank is the love of your life."

"No, baby. It's you." I prop him up on the pillows.

"I'm hideous."

"Never." I sit next to him on the bed, take his head and shoulders in my arms, and rock him. "I love you. I'll always love you." I feel what I'm saying is true.

"There's something I need to tell you." I stop rocking. "Because I have to be honest. Because our relationship is based on honesty." I mouth the words as he's saying them. I look out at the pool. I should just let it go, not press for details. But, as always, I torture myself.

"Esperanza?"

"LaShawna."

"LaShawna?"

"The Fed Ex girl."

"What?" I stand up. "How could you?" Then, looking down at him, I rephrase the question. *"How* could you?"

"Well," he shrugs. "I managed to call you on the phone, didn't I?" He gives me his bad-boy grin. I break down. "Oh, Jeanette. I'm sorry. Forgive me. You know I love you. Don't be sad. You have my heart."

In the end the beginning seems unbelievable, something that happened to people who just look like you, but you can't help going there. The blue splash of Gus diving into the pool at the far end, swimming the length underwater, pulling himself out, lying on top of me on the deck, drenching me.

"You make me feel so beautiful."

"You'd be beautiful with or without me."

"No, it's you."

"This is an affair, Jeanette."

"This is different."

"I'll go the way of the director, the trainer, the redneck, and the pool boy."

"I wasn't in love with any of them." He puts his mouth over mine to quiet me.

We start quarreling immediately upon my return from the *Pretty Mom* awards. "I see I've been replaced." Gus's voice comes up behind me as I'm collecting the last of his teeth and a few skin flaps off the floors and counters. An eye floating in a glass of milk follows me around the kitchen.

"It's not what you think." I go out on the deck.

"Yeah, right." His voice follows as I move to the end of the pool to check the thermostat. "I told you we were doomed."

"Austin took me to the ceremony. He's having his place done. There's dust an inch thick."

"You've seen his place?"

"I still love you."

I hear the shower turn off, Austin Kairys humming the "Battle Hymn of the Republic," the sound of him switching on my hair dryer.

"He's wearing my robe. He's drinking my scotch. That son-of-a-bitch."

"Leave him alone. He has a blood vessel abnormality." I chase Gus's voice through the sliding doors off the bedroom.

"Get out!" Gus yells. "Get out of my house."

"Huh?" Austin calls over the roar of the dryer.

"Get out of my robe! Stop touching my things!"

I pull up behind the voice and open my mouth. Austin switches off the dryer and looks at me.

"Say something, love?"

"Get the f—"

I take in a tremendous breath and swallow. Gus's accusations and recriminations shoot down my gullet like rocket debris hurtling through space.

"Nothing," I say to Austin. A haywire gas bubble bounces off the walls of my stomach. I throw back a shot of Austin's scotch. "Nothing."